DISCOVERED

But still, there was no danger. Partly to keep himself occupied, Jack was exceedingly meticulous about working out the risk of detection statistically. The figures seemed to show that the probability of his being discovered by the Angels was very low.

Jack decided to forge ahead. It took him half a day to record the tape; only then did he turn to setting up the equipment. He was almost ready to turn the switch when the bobbing of the needle caught his eye.

There was a small, intensely radiating body nearby. With his heart in his throat, Jack set the outside scanner going.

But it didn't matter now. He had *already* been discovered.

JAMES BLISH

THE STAR DWELLERS

▲ **AVON**
PUBLISHERS OF BARD, CAMELOT, DISCUS AND FLARE BOOKS

AVON BOOKS
A division of
The Hearst Corporation
959 Eighth Avenue
New York, New York 10019
Copyright © 1961 by James Blish

Introduction Copyright © 1982 by Avon Books.
Published by arrangement with The Estate of James Blish
Library of Congress Catalog Card Number: 81-68857
ISBN: 0-380-57976-6

First Avon Printing, February, 1982

AVON TRADEMARK REG. U. S. PAT. OFF. AND IN OTHER
COUNTRIES. MARCA REGISTRADA. HECHO EN U. S. A.

Printed in the U. S. A.

WFH 10 9 8 7 6 5 4 3 2 1

FORWARD

FOR MANY YEARS, scientists have been seeking to understand the secret of life. As is often the case in the sciences, they began their search with a definition—but it is hard to define something you don't understand, and a good definition of life has proven to be a highly elusive goal.

Eventually, however, most biologists agreed that nothing could be said to be alive unless it showed all of a list of twelve characteristics. (Later the list was expanded to twenty.) For instance, it must be able to reproduce itself. It must grow by taking in materials unlike itself, and changing them into the materials it needs—not by addition from outside, the way a crystal grows in a solution. It must mutate, or show changes in form or other qualities that thereafter breed true. It must be irritable—by which they didn't mean that all living things are bad-tempered, but simply that they show reactions to any prods they get from the world around them.

Decades of careful observation seemed to prove, too, that only one kind of substance fitted all of these conditions: protoplasm, the enormously complex material of which all living cells are made, whether the cells belong to a begonia, a worm or a man. Thus the list got a new proviso, implied rather than stated directly: All life is protoplasmic.

Then came the discovery of the filterable viruses, and this whole beautiful structure came down in ruins.

The viruses are particles so small that only a few of them can be seen with the ordinary laboratory microscope. Most of them have to be photographed at great magnification with the electron microscope; were you to magnify a housefly as much, it would be more than a mile long. They are extremely important to man, because they cause a good many stubborn diseases, including measles, mumps, poliomyelitis, influenza and the common cold. They also attack animals and plants.

They are not protoplasmic. Many of them are made of

chemicals also found in protoplasmic cells, but all of them are a great deal simpler than protoplasm itself. Some of them seem to be made of only a single chemical compound; protoplasm contains thousands.

They do not reproduce themselves. Instead, they enter a living cell and force the cell to manufacture new viruses. All by itself, a virus cannot produce offspring.

They do not take in nourishment, and most of them never grow. They stay as they are when the living cell first turns them out. The exceptions are certain viruses which are simple chemical compounds, like the one which attacks the tobacco plant; these can be produced in the laboratory in crystal form, just like rock salt or rock candy, and the crystals can be made large enough to be seen with the naked eye. No other form of life grows like that, and it seems that the "individual" tobacco mosaic virus, if we can realistically imagine that one exists, must be one single molecule of the chemical involved.

Nevertheless, viruses do meet some of the other definitions of life. They do mutate—which is why new and different vaccines must be produced for almost every epidemic of flu. In fact, they seem to mutate faster than most other organisms. And they are certainly sensitive to their environment: they respond to the presence of a living cell by attacking it and taking control of it, and furthermore they do it selectively—the flu virus never attacks tobacco-plant cells, and tobacco mosaic never attacks potatoes.

One eminent scientist puts it that the virus lives a borrowed life—borrowed from the cell it invades. But there is no doubt that it is alive, however badly it fits the old definitions in some ways.

Obviously the old definitions had somehow missed the point, and a new one had to be found. The new definition finally emerged from a most unexpected source: the science of thermodynamics, the study of the behavior of energy.

One of the basic laws of thermodynamics says that whenever one form of energy is changed into another—for instance, when the mechanical motion of a water wheel is changed by a dynamo into electricity—a tiny fraction of the total energy is permanently lost. This effect is called *entropy*, and it seems to be one of the most basic and fundamental properties of the universe, from the atom to the star.

But it does not appear to apply to life. Though the living cell obviously loses a little energy in each individual energy transaction which goes on within it, somehow the total organism does not; in fact, it actually manages to *gain* a little energy. At the moment of death this ability is lost.

Life, then, is negative entropy . . . entropy running backwards.

This deceptively simple explanation holds just as true for a virus as it does for a protoplasmic creature such as man. We know of no good reason why still other kinds of structures could not behave in the same way. If they did, no matter how bizarre and unlikely they seemed to us, we would be forced to admit that they were alive—just as alive as we are.

Which brings us to Jack Loftus and his peculiar friend Hesperus.

"Arrowhead"   JAMES BLISH
Milford, Pennsylvania
1961

THE STAR DWELLERS

LUCIFER IS FALLEN

THE SUNLIGHT WAS bright indeed in the Washington office of Daniel Hart, Secretary for Space; but this was one of those days when Jack Loftus found it dreamlike, all the same. Of course he had spent a certain amount of his time in high school thinking about how great it would be to be important, in one way or another. He had even thought a little about what changes he would make in the world if he were given the chance.

But he had had better sense than to expect to make it before long years had passed—his father had pounded that into him with a mercilessness which had been none the less stern because it was kind. Yet here he was, at seventeen . . .

"To begin with," Hart was saying, "there's the fact that the capture and subsequent employment of this alien critter—what do they call it, Lucifer?—may very well look like abduction and slavery to the other Angels. Angels! I loathe that name, but I guess we're stuck with it."

"Probably," Langer agreed. He picked up a model of one of the two ships the Angels had destroyed, and turned it around thoughtfully in his hands. "It's pretty hard to give an animal made of pure energy any sort of Latin name out of natural history. For one thing there hasn't been time. And nicknames have a way of sticking, no matter how inappropriate they are."

"Um," Hart said petulantly. He was a tall, careworn man with an iron face and steel-gray hair. He watched Langer with grim concentration, his hands folded together on top of his desk so tightly that all the tendons stood out. Langer, sitting next to him, looked as cherubic and unworried as ever; though he was Hart's top field agent and trouble shooter, nobody could have looked more untroubled.

Jack was not fooled. He had already had time to see Langer at work. The more innocent he looked, the more worried he was— and the more likely to come up with some solution to the current problem so drastic as to throw the whole Department for Space into an uproar of orders, counterorders, and thumbing of lawbooks in search of precedents.

In the single year that Jack had held his coveted position as senior foreign service cadet in Secretary Hart's department, he had come to have a solid respect for Howard Langer. He looked as lazy as a porcupine—and was just as dangerous a critter to blunder against. A large number of shady operators who had fancied their own shrewdness had so blundered, and had been hauled away to the pokey with quills sticking out all over them. When Langer was on the job the best arguments never turned out to be on the side of the devil, regardless of the proverb.

"All the same," Hart was saying, "whatever we call them, they can obviously be deadly when aroused. They've destroyed two ships without any real effort."

"Yes. Speaking of which, what's keeping McCrary?"

"Don't know; I'll check." Hart snapped open the intercom. Out of it at once came a recorded voice, muttering over and over:

"Calling Paul X. McCrary, yacht 2546-2. Department for Space calling McCrary yacht 2546-2. Official. Official. Calling. . . ."

Jack recognized the voice: it belonged to Secretary Hart's underclerk for communications, R. Dover Bearing, usually called "Timkin." He was a brilliant and desperately overworked young man who at nineteen—only two years older than Jack himself, hard though it was to realize it—already seemed to be pushing thirty-five.

Hart leaned forward and pushed a button. "Tim!" he said, explosively. "Haven't you even gotten an acknowledgment yet?"

Almost at once the record faded back a little, and Tim Bearing's real voice came in. The effect was eerie, almost as though he were singing a duet with himself.

"No, sir, not yet. Not even a carrier wave. And somehow he got off without filing a flight plan."

"All right, keep trying."

"Mr. Secretary, if you're not even getting a carrier wave from McCrary's yacht, he's obviously still traveling on the Standing Wave," Langer said indolently. "Until he snaps off it, Tim's tape can shout itself hoarse and McCrary won't hear a word."

"I know that, Major," Hart said. Jack had yet to figure out what military service Howard Langer might belong to, or had once belonged to. Nearly everyone in officialdom seemed to address him by a different rank. Careless people seeking favors called him "Howie," as did the press. His friends called him "Howard." In formal sessions—for instance, before committees and the General Assembly—he was always "Doctor Langer." "But it's a sure sign that we're going to have trouble with the man. I don't care how much money he's got; going beyond Jupiter without filing a flight plan is a breach of the law. And I hate to have to throw that at him now—it's pretty minor compared to our present business with him."

"Oh, I don't know, Dan. It's usually helpful to have a loose lever lying around."

"Um. I leave that to you. Let's get back to the Angels."

"I don't mind," Langer said mildly. "But I don't make policy, Dan. I only carry it out. So far, I don't know what your policy is going to be."

"You read my position paper."

"Pap. Excuse me, Jack—I know you wrote most of it, I recognized your style by the third sentence—but it's only a summary. It doesn't actually take any position at all; and that's not Jack's fault, Dan. He did very well with what he had. But you weren't supposed to be taking a position for the newspapers; you were supposed to be taking it for me. There's a difference."

"I know, I know," the Secretary grumbled. "I did the best I could with what *I* had, too. But it's not adequate."

"Are you sure not? Are you sure that you didn't leave more in Jack's hands than he's supposed to handle? That's always a temptation when you've got a gifted cadet, Dan. Let's hear it again."

"We've already heard it four times!"

"Gently, gently," Langer said. "I want you to listen to it until you hear something in it that sounds like *you,* not like Jack, otherwise I can't act in your behalf. Jack's no more in a position to make policy than I am. You're supposed to do that. And Dan, until you do, my hands are utterly tied."

"Oh, all right. Jack, give it to us again."

Jack opened the folder. By now he was himself more than a little bored with the position paper on the Angels which his sponsor and teacher had had him write for Langer. The trouble shooter's insistence on hearing it read over and over again baffled him, and certainly did not match his previous impression of the swashbuckling Doctor/Major/Mister Langer, who sailed off into danger at a moment's notice and came back with scalps. Yet Langer's whole attention was now focused on him, and the Secretary had ordered him to read the paper yet again, so there was no choice but to go back over the familiar words yet once more.

"The existence of intelligent races on other planets is no longer a novelty to humanity," he read, trying to keep his voice from singsonging. "The ruins and artifacts of the long-dead peoples of Mars were among the first and most exciting discoveries of spaceflight. Since the discovery of the interstellar drive, we have found living intelligent races almost as advanced as we are—though by no means so advanced as the ancient Martians were at the time of their suicide—living on planets of the stars Tau Ceti and 40 Eridani. Lesser races have been found on one of the three colony planets of Earth, and since the oldest of these colonies has been established only five years, we may expect that evidence—"

"Yes, all right, Jack," Langer interrupted. "I don't think we really need the history now—that's what I mean by 'pap.'"

Evidently Jack looked troubled, for Langer's expression softened at once. "I didn't mean to abort your conclusion, Jack. But Secretary Hart made you write all that stuff only to prove that 'Where intelligence *can* arise, it *will* arise.' Finding it on five planets out of the first suitable seven we studied—counting the Earth, of course—proves it beyond a shadow of a doubt, and that's exactly what we expected. Let's get on to the knotty parts."

Jack suppressed a shrug. Though he was a little stung by being cut off in mid-reading, the words no longer seemed very golden to him, regardless of the fact that he had written them; in fact, they were becoming darned dull. He skipped three pages and went on:

"Nevertheless we must confess that the situation in the Coal Sack is surprising. Tentative exploration of this great dark nebula, one of the great interstellar dust clouds which obscures Earth's view of the center of our Milky Way galaxy, was undertaken for the first time last year by three ships of the McCrary Fleet under government sponsorship: the *Lancet*, the *Probe* and the *Electrode*, a coordinated squadron sailing under the general title of—"

"Jack, please, that stuff doesn't matter either. Cut it as you go along."

"Yes, sir. Um . . . On the edge of the Coal Sack the McCrary flight encountered a life form of a completely unprecedented nature: a stable, self-contained electromagnetic field, rather like

14

Earthly ball lightning, capable of moving as freely through empty space as a bird flies in the air or a fish swims in the sea. Apparently these creatures tend to cluster—or perhaps nest—near the stars which are imbedded in this dust cloud; but also they often congregate on the surfaces of the rare, barren planets of these stars—"

"Dan, are you sure of this ball-lightning analogy?" Langer said.

"No, in fact it's Jack's. It's as good as any other, though, it seems to me; otherwise I'd have taken it out."

"Aha. Well, I guess I agree. Okay, Jack, proceed."

"In appearance these creatures are described as being glowing droplets of intense light, four to seven feet in diameter," Jack read. "They are translucent and blood-red when at rest, but they often change color, from a deep orange to a bright canary-yellow. They seem to have complex internal structures, but since these keep changing from second to second, it is difficult to imagine what kind of internal economy they may have. If it is as complicated as that of protoplasm, we may need centuries to understand it."

"Is that your point, Jack? Doesn't sound like it, somehow."

"No, Dr. Langer," Jack said. "I'm no biologist. I got it from the labs."

"Thought so; didn't sound like your boss, either. No discredit to you. Plow on."

"The McCrary Fleet attracted large numbers of these beings," Jack read. "They seemed to know at once what the ships were, at least in general terms, and opened communications at once. These conversations, conducted by radio, were of the most simple kind at first, limited to exchanges of number tables, universal constants like the value of *pi,* and other primerlike material. Nevertheless, they had the value of establishing beyond all doubt that the creatures were intelligent, as well as alive. Up until that point, the captains of the McCrary Fleet had assumed that they were only a local electrical condition, peculiar to the Coal Sack.

"As soon as the two parties began to talk together, however, each of the ships of the McCrary Fleet was boarded by one of the energy-creatures. We do not have a good account of how this was accomplished, but it appears that each creature seemed to soak through the hull of the ship that it boarded, like a drop being absorbed by a sponge. Promptly thereafter, the *Lancet* exploded; the ship was totally destroyed, with all hands. The

15

Probe was disabled and presumably has fallen into the Coal Sack and can be considered lost. The *Electrode* experienced a number of peculiar effects in its driving machinery, which are still being studied, but managed to leave the area and return to Earth . . ."

". . . and to McCrary," Langer said sleepily. "Trouble, trouble. But never mind: Fare forward, Jack—where thy dreams of yore/in splendor drape the fetid shore,/and pestilential waters dead."

"Leave him alone," Hart said, with unexpected sharpness. "It's not his fault that I'm no stylist. Judging by that sample, you're not, either."

"True and beautiful. I apologize. Jack?"

"There's not much left now, but I'd get through it faster if I could read it all at one clip."

"Go ahead," the Secretary said. "Howard, shut up."

"Yes, Your Excellency."

Jack read: "During the flight of the *Electrode* back to Earth, the officers of the vessel became aware that the Coal Sack creature was still with them, occupying the heart of the ship's fusion reactor and tampering with it. The captain of the *Electrode* promptly shut down the fusion reactor and made the rest of the trip home on power derived from his auxiliary fission pile; but the effect of this was to trap the Coal Sack creature inside the fusion chamber and make it a prisoner.

"Since it did not appear feasible either to let the creature go or to try to destroy it, in our present state of ignorance of their powers, the captain and crew of the *Electrode* made a careful study of it—a project facilitated by the length of their journey home on emergency power. In this they were helped by an apparently friendly and co-operative attitude on the part of the creature itself, so that they were soon able to talk to it quite freely.

"In the course of this study it became apparent that the explosion of the *Lancet* and the disabling of the *Probe* would probably have to be considered accidents, rather than hostile acts. The invasion of the three ships of the McCrary Fleet by the three Coal Sack creatures appears to have been a tropism; they were drawn to the ships by the 'glow' of their fusion reactors, much as a cat might settle down next to the fireplace. This conclusion is partially verified by a daring experiment conducted by the crew of the *Electrode*, who partially activated their ship's fusion reactor to make their strange guest more comfortable. In turn, this being proceeded to demonstrate the many feats of control it can exert over raw fusion energy; apparently it can handle this torrent of power with micrometric precision, once it is familiar with the 'fireplace' it is asked to live in."

"An odd analogy," Langer said, pinching the tip of his nose reflectively. "But maybe it's just. I'm still groping, I'm afraid. Read on, Jack."

Jack read: "We now know that these energy-creatures are at home in many kinds of high-energy situations, and indeed seem to think of the atmospheres of suns as pleasant places, like swimming pools or other relaxing milieus; they are wholly at home in the most torrential energy-storms we have yet encountered, and in certain senses seem even to feed on them. But beyond that, it appears that the history of these entities stretches all the way back to the first twenty minutes of the creation of the world, or of the whole universe. They never die, and they were born when the universe was born.

"It is not surprising that the scientists aboard the *Electrode* dubbed them the Angels; or that they named their captive Lucifer, who is fallen. The government is exploring the matter and will make an announcement as soon as any additional information becomes available."

"Goody for the government," Langer said, "if I could believe we had enough material to make an announcement from. I must admit that we've about exhausted the resources of that document, Dan. I notice you don't—"

The buzzer sounded and Secretary Hart flipped the switch. "Yes, Tim?"

"Mr. McCrary's just come off the Standing Wave, Mr. Secretary. Spaceport expects him to land in ten minutes and was going to grill him for failure to file a flight plan; I told them to drop it and squirt him right over here. Did I overstep?"

"No, that's fine. Now you can turn off that intolerable recording."

"Yes, sir, I already have."

Langer put up a hand as Hart moved to shut off the intercom. "Tim, do you know the whereabouts of Jerry Stevens?"

"Sandbag? Sure, Dr. Langer. Shall I put out a call?"

"Please."

Sandbag Stevens was Langer's cadet understudy, as Jack was Secretary Hart's. He was already almost as notorious for getting out of tough scrapes as was Langer himself, though quite frequently he had to be hauled out by the scruff. In addition to brains, he had unlimited amounts of audacity, a quality of high survival value in Langer's kind of job. That he also seemed to have almost no judgment, sometimes even very little common sense, did not seem to ruffle Langer in the least.

"I was saying that your position paper doesn't mention the fact that our captive Angel is now working for a living," Langer resumed.

"No," the Secretary said, "because that situation may not last beyond this meeting. I'm hoping that we can get McCrary to turn Lucifer over to us for study, at least for a while. It's certainly far too early to be letting him wander about the Earth at will, let alone run a fusion generator for a commercial company."

"I've never met McCrary," Langer said, "but I suspect that he's not going to yield the point very easily. However, this at last gives me an idea as to what I can do about all this."

"Good!" Hart said explosively. "I knew I could count on you, Howard. Let's hear it. Oh, *hassenpfeffer.*"

For a split second Jack thought this was simply one of the Secretary's sneezes, which in hay fever season could run to eight or ten syllables and come out in any one of as many languages; but it was only an expletive. Hart hit the intercom button. "Yes, Tim?"

"Mr. McCrary is here," Tim Bearing's voice said, in the rather hollow tone which indicated that he was using the hush mike. "He has a reporter from Trans-Stellar Press with him."

"Well, send McCrary in, and tell the reporter we've got nothing to say to the press yet. I'm surprised at you, Tim."

"Sir, the reporter is Mr. McCrary's daughter, and he insists that she accompany him."

"*Holzblaeser,*" the Secretary said. This time it was *definitely* not a sneeze. "All right, send them in."

MISSION TO A NEBULA 2

IT HAD BEEN a long journey from the enormous California truck farm where Jack Loftus had spent his boyhood, to the office of the Secretary for Space in Washington, and Jack still found it hard to believe that it had all taken place in so few years. He had of course been lucky to grow up in a community which had pioneered the new, accelerated high school curriculum and was now comfortable with it. He had been luckier still to be kept in the V Class, in which students were advanced as fast as they proved able to go, regardless of the mechanics of semesters and school years. But it had always seemed to him that he would go on to college to study space law, as his father had done; that was a settled thing in his mind.

Then had come the evening when his father had said to him, as casually as though talking about nothing of any consequence at all:

"Jack, have you ever thought of becoming a foreign service cadet?"

"Why—no, Dad. Come to think of it, I never knew there was such a thing."

"There is. It's a branch of space law, essentially. Terrestrial foreign service requires men who have spent a lifetime in the diplomatic service, and somebody in the last administration had the good sense to realize that in space law, even a lifetime might not be enough—as a 'lifetime' used to be defined. So the Department of Space is catching them young."

"How young?"

"Your age. It wouldn't have been possible under the old educational system, but the assumptions have changed radically since the 1960's—and high time, too. Did you know that in the old days a boy your age didn't know the calculus?"

"They *didn't?*" Jack said ungrammatically. "How can you even drive a car without knowing that?"

"Lots of people did. It was suicidal, but they did; the law allowed it. But the country got into technological competition with the Soviet Union, which was very good for both sides. Over here we were forced to admit that a child can be given knowledge in almost unlimited quantities, far faster than the then-current educational system was taking advantage of. By the age of seventeen, a bright youngster can be a thoroughly trained technician in the most difficult of disciplines, if he has the will and is given sufficient push and opportunity."

"They do push," Jack and ruefully.

"Sure they do. It pays. In the old days, though, they had the notion that education ought to be painless—which is also a suicidal notion, if ever I heard one. Well, the cadet system evolved out of the forced-feed curriculum. The assumption is that knowledge is no substitute for judgment; that comes only through experience. The most gifted youngsters in their fields are apprenticed to top adult practitioners in those fields, and their judgment is force-matured as fast as possible—often by throwing them into sink-or-swim situations. It's pretty grueling; in the foreign service, it takes ten years. But at the end of two years, if you make it that far, you're apprenticed to an actual, operating foreign service officer of some stature, and shortly thereafter you may go into space. That opportunity strikes very seldom, elsewhere in space law, which is mostly pretty bound to the courts."

Mr. Loftus did not need to say more on that point. Though it was seldom discussed, Jack knew that his father, though one of the most scholarly men in his field, had been into space only once throughout his career—a hard fate for a man who had dreamed of the stars since he had been old enough to know that they were suns.

"Well—I don't know what to say. Of course I'd like it. How do I go about it?"

"There's a competitive examination at Vallejo in two months. If you'd like to enter, I'll coach you for it. It won't be easy."

"Hmm." Jack had been through his father's coaching before. It was, to say the least, anything but easy, even when it was interesting. But—

"Dad, is this a scholarship deal?"

"No," Mr. Loftus said. "The government regards it as a privilege and expects the parents of the cadet to pay the freight—that is, the testing costs, transportation and so on— just as we would for any first-class college. If you get through the first two years and are apprenticed to an operating officer, thereafter you're on the Federal payroll, just like your superior. But I expect you'll feel worse if you fail at Vallejo than you would if you failed to get a scholarship."

Jack frowned. "I'd feel even worse," he said, "if I didn't even try."

"That's what I thought you'd say, but I'm pleased to be proven right. The fact is, Jack, I don't expect you to fail."

"What about Mother?"

"Well?"

"I mean, these 'sink-or-swim' situations—either some of them are dangerous, or they aren't really 'sink-or-swim.' Does she know that?"

"No," Mr. Loftus said, "she doesn't. But by the time you encounter one, you will have been out of the nest more than two years, which should be sufficient. You leave that to me; it's wholly my responsibility, not yours. Now pull Volume One of *Samachson on Orbits* from the middle shelf, will you? We had better get started."

Jack did not fail at Vallejo; but the first elation passed quickly, when he realized that passing meant only that he was undertaking a series of relentless tests which would last a solid ten years more. Even his selection as Secretary Hart's understudy was as sobering as it was gratifying—for if you fail the Secretary for Space, you fail more than a test; you may fail to do right by the whole Earth. Jack had moments of thinking that the system was downright crazy; but he had a chance to observe how the cadets in classes ahead of him bore up under it, and how they served their native planet in the clinches, and he had to admit that thus far there had been no important breakdowns—not even with Sandbag Stevens, wild though he seemed to be.

He lived with the nightmare that the first failure of the system—and the last failure for Earth—might be Jack Loftus.

Paul X. McCrary, of McCrary Engineering to begin with, but with ties to so many other corporations that only the Treasury and McCrary's own accountant had the data to unscramble them, was a bristle-haired bulky Irishman with a manner of surface cheerfulness and an undercurrent of gutter toughness which suggested that he might put out one of your eyes for disagreeing with him, or maybe just for the fun of it—the kind of a man who might have been president of a dock-wallopers' union in the old days, before the unions became just another kind of corporation. In Secretary Hart's office he seemed even more to belong to an earlier century, but he looked no less dangerous to Jack for all that. Hart, to judge by his taut reserve, felt the same way. Only Langer seemed to be at ease and unimpressed, and Jack was suddenly seized by the notion that a battle between McCrary and Langer would be a real doozer . . . despite the fact that Langer was both smaller and softer to the casual eye.

"We were just talking about you," Langer said. "And your new employee—Lucifer."

"Naturally, naturally, Howie, that's why you brought me here. Gentlemen, my daughter Sylvia, a probationary reporter for the Trans-Stellar Press. About the same age as this young man, I would guess."

"The young man is John Loftus, my understudy. Miss McCrary, I'm Secretary Hart, and this is Dr. Howard Langer."

Sylvia nodded, looking faintly amused, which for some reason rather irritated Jack. Though she had black hair, she was very fair and had blue eyes, and was most neatly put together; a real four-alarm distraction, which Jack found himself resenting. No reporter belonged in this meeting, not even a probationary one, nor would she have gotten past the door had it not been for her father's insistence.

She caught Jack looking at her and nodded distantly. This did not improve his temper. He looked stonily away toward Secretary Hart.

"I took my daughter with me to Titan in the hope that it might give her a story," McCrary said effusively. "We're opening a mine there; you know, local color, that sort of thing. But she said it was old stuff. We parents get outdated quickly. Sit down, Sylvia. Your Excellency, how may I help you?"

"Well," the Secretary said, "this is a closed meeting, Mr. McCrary. I hope your daughter understands that."

"Of course, of course." But Jack saw Sylvia's eyes flash for an instant. "Since we're dealing with Lucifer, it's a family matter, so to speak; not for the press. Let's proceed. I've just had a longish trip and I'm a little tired."

"We understand that. Very well. First of all, Mr. McCrary, this office has prepared a position paper which we'd like you to read; that will save us a lot of time."

Jack passed the well-thumbed paper to McCrary, who read it at astonishing speed; he seemed to be not so much reading it as eating it. He handed the sheets back to Jack, without looking at him, in a rumpled jumble.

"An able presentation. I have no objections. What next?"

"Doesn't it strike you that there's something missing?" Langer said curiously.

"Oh, certainly. I presume that was by intention. What do you gentlemen want me to do—tell you how I see the subsequent events?"

"That would be a good start," Langer agreed. "It would be the fastest way of giving us your point of view."

"Um. All right. If the young man takes dictation—"

"Mr. Loftus is my understudy, not my secretary," Hart said. "Just throw it out and we'll record. You may review the tape before it's transcribed."

"Aha. Very good. Well then, gentlemen, I ought to start by reminding you that Squadron Surgeon—the *Probe* and her companion vessels—is privately owned. They belong to McCrary Engineering, which is one of four large stockholder corporations specifically organized to exploit space travel and its by-products—expected and unexpected—for profit. The government has acknowledged our right to do so, and blessed it; it rightly recognizes that unless space travel eventually produces income of some kind, it will die of its inherently huge costliness."

"No argument there," Secretary Hart said. "It's not a proper function of government to seek profits, or to tax citizens for red-ink operations like interstellar flight when there's no return visible. Jack?"

"Salem vs. Uscott, Mars District Two, *amicus curiae* the Government of Belgium, *et seq.*"

"Right as rain. Go on, Mr. McCrary."

"Gladly. I only wanted to establish that the crew of the *Electrode* had every right to see in their captured Angel the germ of a profit-making situation. They are employees of a privately owned company which is not only empowered but enjoined to make profits. Now: I can tell you, if Dr. Langer doesn't know it already, that fusion power generators are still much bulkier than we wish they were, and still enormously tricky to operate, even after a century of commercial development. But with one of these Angels, like Lucifer, to exercise the actual control functions, some eighty per cent of the usual reactor can simply be trimmed off and discarded, or turned to some other use.

"If this were to become a general practice—if we had that many Angels to use—it would turn the generation of electricity by fusion from a marginally profitable operation to an immensely profitable one, even allowing for the reductions in the price per kilowatt hour for power so generated, upon which the Public Service Commission would certainly insist. I don't want to get into *that* argument, not at any rate right now.

"And Lucifer has agreed to take on the job. That's where we stand as of this moment. Any quibbles?"

"Doesn't it scare you?" Langer said quietly. "One of his fellows has already proven that he could easily detonate a fusion reactor, probably at no hurt to himself. Supposing he were to lose his temper some day?"

"A bogey," McCrary scoffed. "What could make him angry? He considers it a privilege to visit us and study us, and a fusion reactor is a convenient place to feed—saves him the trouble of having to visit the Sun every few weeks."

"What indeed? We don't know, and that's exactly my point. Until we know positively what does make him angry we have to assume that almost anything might."

"Poppycock."

Langer was spared having to reply to this pre-symbolic snarl by the buzzer. "Dr. Langer," Tim's voice said, "your understudy is here."

"Why," Sylvia said as the rangy blond cadet entered, "it's Sandbag Stevens! How have you been since the big dust-up in New Chicago?"

"Hello, Sylvia. This is the last place I expected to see you again."

"You know this man, Sylvia?" McCrary said suspiciously. "How does that happen?"

"I had a little trouble during the New Chicago riots, some months ago, sir," Sandbag said, a little embarrassed. Jack was not surprised at the embarrassment, for it was in New Chicago that Sandbag had earned his nickname. "Sylvia covered the riots for Trans-Stellar. Covering the Angels story, I suppose?"

"Trying to," Sylvia said. "But I'm not having much luck at—"

"Sylvia, you can prosecute your social life later," her father growled. "I'm here on business."

This had the effect of reminding Sandbag that he too was there on business. Flushing, he came to attention before Langer and saluted. "Excuse me, sir. Cadet Stevens reporting."

"Rest, Jerry. Better start by reading that little essay Jack over there is holding. I think you know everything in it, but better be sure." Sandbag nodded, sat next to Jack and began to read. "As I was saying, Mr. McCrary, I don't take too kindly to this business. We don't know how the other Angels will take it, and they can obviously be deadly when aroused. Or if everything goes superficially well, our planet may wind up dotted with fusion generators under the sole real control of the Angels, which would be giving them the drop on us with a vengeance. I don't believe in inviting a potential enemy into my household and putting him in charge of the family shotgun."

"How could they possibly be potential enemies?" McCrary said with obvious exasperation. "We don't have a thing they want or even could use—they're space-dwelling critters, not planet-bound like us."

"Mr. McCrary, I can appreciate your position," Secretary Hart put in soothingly. "You are an official of the holding company involved; if I understand your statement correctly,

24

you are both a member of the board, and McCrary Engineering is one of the four corporations which make up the complex. Yes? In the latter capacity, you're obviously eager to see the loss of two of your ships in the Coal Sack expedition recouped by whatever benefit can be made to accrue from the expedition, for the complex as a whole. Otherwise both the board and the stockholders may have you on the carpet."

Sylvia laughed musically, distracting Sandbag from his reading. "Dad, you ought to commit that to memory. It couldn't be better if your public relations chief had written it for you."

"Sylvia, please. It's true, Mr. Secretary, you've summarized my situation very well."

"Then I ask you to consider that my job in turn compels me to entertain all the possible legal and diplomatic knots in this matter. One of the things I must bear in mind is that nobody can yet be sure whether or not Lucifer always tells the truth. Intelligent beings seldom do, and indeed often can't afford to. In my opinion it would be best to have some kind of thorough diplomatic accord with the Angels as a whole—that is, as a race or nation or whatever they are—before the experiment is allowed to become wholesale and involve the whole economy, and the life or death of millions of people."

One of the abilities Jack most envied in the Secretary was his ability to weave complex sentences from a standing start and come out properly untangled at the end of each. One kind of assistant Hart would never need was a ghost writer.

"Now that we know where we stand," Langer added, "I have a proposal to offer. Mr. McCrary, I don't know if you've heard of the cruiser assigned to me, the *Ariadne*; she's a super-fast, stripped-down job especially fitted out for my use. I'd like to take it to the Coal Sack and attempt preliminary new contacts with the Angels."

"Uhmm. What for, may I ask?"

"Primarily to get more information—preferably from some source other than Lucifer. From the utterances of his I've read about so far, I suspect him of having a decidely *outré* sense of humor. At the same time, I can attempt to do whatever is left to be done for the disabled McCrary ship still out there, the *Probe*. How does this strike everyone? I mean to imply, of course, that we keep Lucifer unemployed until I get back."

"I concur; a very useful-sounding move," Hart said promptly.

"Uhmm. I'd rather see Lucifer put to work at once, at least on an experimental basis," McCrary said. "In fact I would be for sending out more ships to pick up more Angels to work for us on the same terms. On the other hand, the bare possibility of salvaging the *Probe* is of course attractive to me, especially if you are to be the man to undertake it, Dr. Langer. I know your reputation—everybody does."

"I don't promise anything so grandiose as salvage," Langer pointed out. "If it's possible I'll salvage the vessel, of course. But it depends on what I find."

"Naturally. Well . . . all right. So long as you in turn understand that I won't be stalled a second time."

"Good. Jerry, go commission the *Ariadne* pronto-pronto, and do all the necessary dirty work; I'll join you shortly."

"Yes, *sir*," Sandbag said, thrusting the position back into Jack's hands. "I'd polish all the asteroids with a soft cloth to get off these training assignments. See you later, Sylvia."

McCrary watched him go with an expression abruptly turned flinty. When the door closed behind Sandbag, he said:

"Do I understand correctly, Dr. Langer, that you are planning to take this green youngster with you?"

"He's a youngster, but he's not green; he's my understudy," Langer said. "I can't offhand think of a better assignment for him at this point in his training. There's no doubt that he's headstrong—as you obviously gathered from your daughter's remarks—and has gotten into a scrape or two in the past. But in a job where improvisation and initiative are essential, like mine, that's a positive advantage."

"Hear, hear!" Sylvia said enthusiastically. Her father gave her what could only be described as a dirty look.

"One other thing, Dan," Langer said. "I have a feeling that we may need to split the party at some time during the negotiations; call it a hunch. And if I'm away I *don't* want Jerry in charge of anything that involves diplomatic formalities; he may never be good at those as long as he lives. Could you spare me, Jack, do you think?"

Jack's heart nearly stopped on the spot.

"Well," the Secretary said slowly, "in about a month we have another matter coming up where I'll have to have him on tap. But knowing you, Howard, I suspect that this affair will be successfully concluded by then. Yes; I'll transfer him to you temporarily as of today."

"The whole proposition seems perfectly and completely harebrained to me," McCrary growled. "Children, on a mission of this much gravity!"

"Foreign service cadets," Langer said, "are not children. Are you sure that that's all that's troubling you?"

"If it weren't, I wouldn't have wasted my breath saying so," McCrary said. "Come on, Sylvia. We have several other fish to fry before nightfall."

"Dad," Sylvia said slowly, "are you sure you're not making a mistake?"

"This is no place to open such a question. Are you coming with me, or are you going to walk home?"

"Two hundred miles? I should say not." She followed him out; but behind his back, she turned once and shrugged expressively. Jack could not help grinning back. Langer merely nodded once, as if thanking her for her politeness in trying to see both sides of the question. The Secretary did not seem to see the shrug at all.

"Mr. McCrary," Langer observed dryly when the door had closed, "seems to be his own worst enemy."

"And maybe the Earth's," Secretary Hart said somberly.

Jack heard the overtones of foreboding in his mentor's voice, and on any other occasion would have been troubled by them; but at this moment he was too full of elation to be dampened by anything.

He was going into space!

INTO THE UNKNOWN   3

IN THE WORLD of 2050, nearly two decades after the discovery of the Haertel faster-than-light drive, the *Ariadne* looked like an anachronism. Interstellar vessels today were huge, and tended to come in a variety of shapes, many of them strongly suggesting something that had been put together from the contents of a vegetable bin. One of the oldest, biggest and most reliable of them was perfectly cubical, and rose from the surface of the Earth to the top of the atmosphere with the gentleness of an elevator—after which she flicked into Haertel overdrive so efficiently that she utterly vanished.

The *Ariadne*, however, was small and streamlined, like a rather fat bullet; her design harked all the way back to the guided missiles and satellite vehicles of the previous century, at the dawn of spaceflight. The reason for this was simple. In the prosecution of his trouble-shooting job, Langer sometimes needed to plow through a thick planetary atmosphere at speeds far above the decorous landing or take-off velocities of modern interstellar ships. He did not want his personal cruiser owning any protuberances or sources of turbulence—not even as small a one as a rivethead—which might melt from atmospheric friction while he was going somewhere in a hurry.

Jack had never seen the *Ariadne* before, though he had been exposed to many pictures of her, and his first sight of her in gleaming, featureless reality made him whistle. Her streamlining was so drastic that she looked as though she were breaking the sound barrier just sitting still on the field.

"She is pretty, isn't she?" Sandbag said. "And in space she's faster than thought. Her Nernst generators are as big as anything you'll find in a liner, even one as big as the *Telemachus*. They take up more than half the space inside."

"Nothing faster in space today," Langer agreed. "But also pretty beastly in an atmosphere; I doubt that the average commercial pilot would ever be able to land her. The first time you tried it solo, Jerry, I thought I'd lost myself a ship *and* an understudy."

"I thought so too," Sandbag confessed. "But I can land her now, more or less."

"You handle her like a baby carriage now, I'll give you that," Langer said, to Sandbag's obvious pleasure. "But we'd better get aboard. I've had her insides rearranged a little since you brought her over here, and I want you both to be thoroughly familiar with her present layout."

Judging by Sandbag's expression after they had boarded the *Ariadne*, "rearranged a little" was a gross understatement of what Dr. Langer had had done to his personal cruiser. Though the control cabin was barely large enough to hold all three of them at once, Sandbag seemed hard put to it to recognize the place.

"There's the autopilot," he said, "and there are the manuals. But what are all these new meters on the right board? And what's that huge locker doing on the back bulkhead? You could put a horse in it, almost."

"That's nothing," Langer said, smiling. "Wait till you see the locker abaft. It lies just under the deck and it runs fore-and-aft almost the whole length of the ship. Furthermore, you can't get into it from inside."

"Dr. Langer, if you mean to baffle me, I can tell you you've made it, hands down."

"No, not really. I just like to make you think once in a while. For instance: all the extra metering on the right board is for cruising the Coal Sack. The inside of that kind of nebula is a constant and furious storm of hard radiation and high-velocity atomic particles. We'll need to keep a constant check on what we're being bombarded with, from minute to minute. So—problem: What's in the new locker, in here?"

"Spacesuits," Sandbag said promptly. "Just like the old locker had. But these are bigger because they need more shielding."

"Precisely. Okay, next question: These facts being so, what has to be in the long locker, abaft?"

Sandbag scratched his head. Finally he said: "You've got me."

"Jack?"

"Sir, I don't have the foggiest notion. I wouldn't even have guessed right on the first question."

"Well, can't blame you for that. This is your first trip in space, and besides you weren't familiar with the old *Ariadne*. All the same I've given you both all the clues you need to answer the second question. Think about it."

"Uh—I suppose you can get into the big locker from outside, on the hull?" Sandbag said after a moment.

"Yes."

"So it's something we might need outside the ship, but not inside."

"It's so big because we couldn't get into it with the bigger spacesuits otherwise?"

"No. You're shooting from the hip, Jerry. Sleep on it a while. Right now I want you both familiarized with these controls—we're leaving tonight."

Jack sucked in his breath. "So soon, sir?"

"Yes; I owe it to the Secretary to prosecute all missions with all possible speed, and this one may well be much tougher than I made it sound in conference. Any objections?"

"Uh, no, sir, not for myself. But I haven't notified my parents yet that—"

"Secretary Hart has already notified your parents. I presume you filed a Last Letter immediately after taking the Oath."

"Yes, sir."

"Then you have fulfilled your duties to your family and your time is now totally the business of the foreign service. Let's get down to cases: we have something under four hours in which to familiarize ourselves with the *Ariadne* in her present state."

He sat down before the boards. Utterly miserable, Jack silently took the observer's post to his left, while Sandbag sat down in the co-pilot's couch.

"Computation drill," Langer said. "Read-and-feed to begin with. When you've both got that, we'll do snap interpretation from the tape against the stop watch. And pay attention; you're both to be proficient by an hour before take-off so you can get in a nap. I'll ground the man who isn't."

It was awful. Sandbag proved to be humiliatingly faster than Jack at almost everything, even taking into account the fact that he had been into space before and knew the basic structure of the *Ariadne*. Jack found himself lost time and time again, and was also distracted by the conviction that he had made a fool of himself the very first time the chips had been put down. As far as he could see, he was incompetent to rub brightwork on a ship of this kind, let alone be part of a select three-man crew.

But when Langer finally put the stop watch back into its clip on the boards, he said only: "All right, Jerry. Jack, you could be better, even for an Earthlubber; but you pass. Now both of you go below and get some shut-eye. I want you fresh when we lift."

Sandbag grinned and stretched. "She's a lot hotter than she ever was before," he said, patting the curve of the hull.

"She's explosively hot, and I don't want any fatigued reflex arcs meddling with any part of her, not even the garbage chute," Langer said grimly. "Be off, or I'll kick you downstairs."

Sandbag went out, not very much abashed. By this time, Jack no longer knew how he felt—and wasn't too sure that he wanted to know.

And as it turned out, neither of them got any sleep at all. Jack was just turning in, in his almost coffin-narrow "cabin," when the whole inside of the *Ariadne* jangled with the bell which meant that somebody was holding down the outside emergency alarm of the airlock. There was no answering summons from Langer to indicate that he wanted his cadets on deck with him, but Jack heard Sandbag's boots strike metal just across the well from him, and got up to follow automatically. Having already once today seemed to be thinking more about himself than about his assignment, Jack was grimly determined to be on tap if needed, whether he was called or not.

But he was quite stunned to discover the control cabin already occupied by Paul X. McCrary and his irritatingly pretty daughter. Since Langer and Sandbag were also there, he was unable to go any farther; all he could do was to stand irresolutely in the open valve. Had he tried to crowd onto the bridge, they would all have been breathing in each other's faces, and forced to change position by maneuvers closely akin to square dancing in slow motion.

"All the same you have no business aboard my ship," Langer was saying, in a voice of glacial cold. "I will give you two and a half minutes to state your business, after which I will ask you to leave or be removed as a sightseer. Unless, of course, you prefer to be called a trespasser."

"I don't think I care for either label," McCrary said. "And it might be as well if you reminded yourself that as a public official you're my employee, and as such owe me a little courtesy. I have no doubt that my taxes alone cover your salary two or three times over."

"No doubt," Langer agreed. "This last observation relieves me of any obligation to act in accordance with the first one, valid though it is. One and a half minutes."

McCrary let it drop; evidently he had realized that no amount of bluster was likely to move Langer an inch. "I came here to do you a favor," he said, still heatedly. "My daughter here has won herself an unlimited press pass to join your mission as an observer—"

"Wholly impossible," Langer said coldly.

"My sentiments precisely," McCrary said, to Jack's surprise. "As her father I have forbidden her to do any such thing, in fact."

"Which you can't do either," Sylvia put in. "My pass is a government recognition, under the apprentice system, that I'm now a skilled adult in my trade. What I can't make you see, Dad, is that I'm not only *allowed* to go—my job *obligates* me to go."

She seemed to be watching Sandbag and Jack out of the corners of her eyes for their reactions. Sandbag was grinning appreciatively; as for Jack, he was sure he looked chagrined, no matter how hard he was trying to keep his face expressionless. It would be seven years more before he was recognized as a skilled adult in *his* trade. He and Sandbag were still only apprentices.

"This is true," McCrary was saying. "If she won't take my advice, I can't prevent her by any legal means. The old arbitrary age criteria don't apply any more, I'm sorry to say. But you can forbid her, Dr. Langer, as the head of the mission."

"Which I do," Langer said promptly. "Though not out of any disapproval of the principle involved. As you can see, this is a small and highly specialized ship. It would be physically impossible to carry another person, unless he had such a high order of the *necessary* skills as to justify his replacing one of my cadets. This clearly doesn't apply to you, Sylvia, regardless of your competence rating as a reporter—for which, by the way, congratulations."

"Thank you," she said, somewhat sullenly. Obviously her moment of triumph over the cadets had been spoiled, but Langer's graciousness would hardly have permitted her to counterattack in her own behalf even if she had been able to. "Well, I know what Trans-Stellar will think of all this. They'll call it censorship."

"That is visibly not the issue at all," Langer said, "as I'm sure you'll be able to point out to them with no difficulty. And now I really must ask you to leave. I've given you more time than I said I would, in view of the fact that you had a more or less legitimate errand; but we have to get ready for take-off."

McCrary nodded and left, brushing by Jack on his way to the airlock without a word. Sylvia followed, but once more she could not resist the opportunity to have the last word. Just as she was about to disappear around the edge of the well, she turned and stuck out her tongue.

The inner valve had no sooner closed than Sandbag burst into an explosion of laughter, in which Jack joined out of sheer relief of tension. Langer's face, however, remained sober.

"Peculiar," he said. "There's more to that than meets the eye."

"How do you mean, sir?" Sandbag said. "I really can't blame the girl. I mean, she's got her certificate, and right away she wants to tackle the toughest job in her line she can dig up. I'd want it that way myself, when the time comes. Of course, maybe she wanted to show off a little for Jack and me, too, but that's understandable."

Jack looked more sharply at Sandbag. This defense of a presumptuous chit of a girl was far from like him; usually girls made him fume with impatience. Had she managed to get under his skin? If it were me, Jack thought uneasily, I'd turn blue before I'd admit it—or even imply it.

Langer may have come to the same conclusion; at least his next remark was: "Jerry, you're aware of the cadet corps' rules about marriage, of course."

"Yes, sir," Sandbag said evenly. "We're to abstain not only from marriage, but from any and all contacts which might lead to marriage, until we have completed training. I assure you, sir, that when I swore to abide by the rules, I meant it."

"Good. I will say no more."

"But sir," Sandbag said, "I'm not required to like it."

To this the trouble shooter made no direct reply. Instead, he began snapping open the switches which started power flowing from the *Ariadne*'s main reactor into the Haertel overdrive.

"Cadets, make all secure. Posts. Take-off in ten minutes."

BUBBLE IN SPACE-TIME   4

THE TAKE-OFF was wholly uneventful, for this time Langer was not sufficiently in a hurry to stage one of his screaming ninety-second ascents of the atmosphere for which the *Ariadne* was so peculiarly designed. Jack was disappointed. History told him that one of Langer's famous take-offs was very much like all take-offs back in the days of chemically powered spaceships, except for the lack of acceleration pressure; but this one, instead, was exactly like the take-off of the over-the-atmosphere rocket which had brought him from California to Washington—seemingly both effortless and gentle.

He should, of course, have expected nothing else, for in both cases the Haertel field was used to cushion the passengers, so that in both cases the real velocities involved were far greater than they were able to feel. His real problem was what he did not properly understand the theory of the Haertel effect, and so couldn't really appreciate the services it was performing for him or see how they were brought about.

He could have given a detailed description of the theory of command, for a knowledge of it was fundamental to interstellar flight and hence to many situations likely to arise in space law. His math was more than good enough to show how the old Lorenz-Fitzgerald expression of Einsteinian relativity, which says that the mass of an object increases and its length decreases as its velocity approaches the speed of light, had been transformed by the twentieth-century British astronomer Milne from a natural law into a simple teaching convenience, eliminating the speed-of-light barrier almost completely; and he could have gone on from there to show how Haertel, by applying something called "Mach's axiom" or "the cosmological assumption," had been able to show that the light-barrier was actually only a sort of local ordinance which disappeared completely if you took the whole mass of the universe into account. This of course involved knowing what the whole mass of the universe was, but the engineers had gotten around that in a very simple way: they had inserted various more-or-less likely values for M into Haertel's equations until they found one that worked, and then ruled that that was automatically the correct figure for the mass of the universe.

Pure theorists were scornful, pointing out that there was a huge hole in the logic; to which the engineers retorted that they didn't care so long as their Haertel overdrive worked—which it certainly did. If their value for M turned out *not* to be a true value for the mass of the universe, then the theorists were going to have an even bigger headache explaining why the overdrive did indeed function, and function superbly, with a wrong value stuck into its heel like a thorn.

In terms of results, the Haertel overdrive turned each ship into a little universe of its own, the Standing Wave—actually not a wave but a sort of bubble in space-time, in which all the cozy local Newtonian ordinances seemed to hold true regardless of how fast the bubble was traveling in relation to the rest of the universe. How fast it "actually" went depended upon how much power you were able to put into the field—a fact the theorists were happy to seize upon, for if the theory were entirely sound the Haertel overdrive ought to be so completely independent of the rest of the universe as to be uncontrollable. It was somewhere in the course of this part of the argument that Jack had gotten lost, or decided that it was entering into realms which could have no useful meaning in space law—he had never been able honestly to decide which consideration had influenced him most. It occurred to him that this would be an excellent time to ask some questions of Langer, who had published three papers about the theory in *Astronautica Acta;* but then he remembered how formidably those papers had bristled with spinor calculus, a discipline which made tensors look as simple as alphabet-blocks, and decided against it with a mental shudder. The mission, after all, would give him more than enough to think about as it was, all directly related to his job as an apprentice diplomat; let the physicists and mathematicians have the theoretical knots to themselves.

It didn't occur to him to wonder why so furiously active a diplomat as Secretary Hart's trouble shooter found those knots well worth bothering with . . . not yet, anyhow.

"That'll do nicely," Langer said, touching a stud. A circuit breaker silently opened, showing only as a tiny yellow lens of light on the board, like a topaz asterisk. "We'll be on automatic until we get out of the Solar system, and then we'll begin to put on some speed. Doesn't pay to pour on much coal before we cross the orbit of Neptune—too much junk floating around—and than we'll still have to pass the cometary shell, which is a good light-year out. After that, we'll go up to cruising speed."

Was the *Ariadne* as fast as that? For the ordinary interstellar ship, "empty" space effectively began just on the other side of the orbit of Jupiter; and even so, it wasn't traveling fast enough by the time it passed through the eggshell of unborn comets—mostly just floating icebergs, left over from the earliest days of creation—to have to worry about hitting one. For the first time Jack began to understand what an inferno of power the *Ariadne* carried, tucked just behind her gently inflected waist.

"How fast are we going now?" he said tentatively.

"I don't know," Langer said, lifting his eyebrows. "It's one of those questions nobody's settled yet. Theoretically we have no velocity at all—or if we do, nobody's devised a ship's instrument to register it."

"Yes, but still there's a crossover, and there's the clock for it right there on the board," Jack objected. "Otherwise we'd never know where we were."

"Perfectly true," Langer said, smiling gently. "But a timer is all it is. It measures elapsed Haertel time, which correlates roughly with elapsed subjective time. For all the sophistications in the books, flight between the stars is still mostly an alarm-clock operation. Speaking of which, I think we'd better settle in. You didn't get your sleep when I wanted you to. You're ordered to do so now—and I defy McCrary or anybody else to interrupt you at this time."

Sandbag yawned; and suddenly Jack too realized that he was trembling on the verge of exhaustion.

"Yes, *sir*," he said.

* * *

Despite all the power that quivered inside the *Ariadne*'s satiny welded skin, the trip to the Coal Sack was a long one; it would involve one stopover for additional supplies of food, water and oxygen. (Not for fuel, however; even at the fantastic rate at which Langer's cruiser expended energy, the Nernst generator would not need to be rebuilt for a solid year.)

This left them all with considerable time on their hands, even subtracting for the drills which Langer required, for much of the operation of the *Ariadne* on a long cruise was automatic. Jack quickly exhausted the wonder of looking out at the stars, for in a ship without ports the only way to see out is via television screen; and Jack had seen the stars-from-space on a television screen since his earliest boyhood, as had all his generation.

Sandbag, however, had no difficulty in filling up the inactive stretches with reams of chatter. He loved to talk, and was good at it; and like most really expert talkers, he was also an excellent listener, every man's new anecdote later becoming one·of his own. Jack was particulary amused by the conversation on the third ship's day, when Sandbag plied Langer with questions about the celibate rule of the cadet corps. It was quite obvious that these had a bearing on Sylvia McCrary, and that Sandbag had found a way to talk about her without apparently mentioning her at all.

"I said I was going to follow the rules as I swore to, and I meant it," he said. "But sir, I don't see the sense of this particular one. Regular officers in the career services marry and don't seem to be any the worse for it. Why be so strict with the cadets?"

"Not all regular officers are so fortunate," Langer pointed out. "For instance, a Space Navy man, or a submariner in the Merchant Marine. They join up knowing that there may be cruises on which they won't see a woman for a year or more. They seem to survive·it, in fact they even become proud of their service under what an outsider might call such unnatural conditions."

"But cadets aren't ordinarily thrown into that kind of situation," Sandbag persisted. "So why insist upon it?"

"Well, Jerry, I don't know how much you know about heuristics—the theory of learning. It all derives ultimately from a gimmick in the brain called *imprinting*. In ducklings, for example, the first twenty-four hours after they're hatched are crucial. The first moving object that they see during that period, they accept as their mother—whether it's a live duck, a rolling

36

ball, or even a man. At the end of that day, you can't imprint a duckling any more—or make it *unlearn* any false impressions it may have gained. Something of the sort takes place in people, too, but in people it goes on for quite a long time.

"While we are teaching you what we want you to know, we want it to stick. This is why we teach you solid geometry and many other rather hard subjects as early in your high school career as we can—at the imprinting age. Once sexual awareness enters the picture (and by that I mean just a simple interest in the fact that there are two sexes), you have encountered a very powerful biological force which heavily interferes with imprinting. We want to cram everything into your head that we can before this period of distraction sets in, because it may be years before you are able to cope with the distraction well enough to continue the learning process. Some men never become able to cope with it, and their brains freeze. Hence the celibate rule. It has precedents, I assure you, which extend many centuries back before imprinting was discovered.

"There doesn't seem to be much doubt that imprinting is a survival from savagery which the race doesn't need any more—just as we no longer need to hold onto trees by our feet. But newborn babies can grip with their feet as well as any chimpanzee, and like it or lump it, the imprinting mechanism is still in our brains too. We can use it, to teach you *now* what you need to know *now*. But to do that, we have to keep you away from the stimulus that most affects the imprinting surfaces of the brain, so the space that's supposed to be occupied by knowledge and skills doesn't get displaced by pin-up pictures, soupy poetry, dismally bad popular music, and all the other props of chain infatuation."

"Wow," said Sandbag, grinning.

"Wow indeed, but you might say it in a softer voice if you'd had to grow up during the last century," Langer said seriously. "In those days they not only allowed these things to compete with learning, but they founded whole industries to cater to them and encourage the worst aspects of them. They poisoned the prints and the air day and night with the stuff, until even the adults couldn't avoid it for most of their lives. And the poisoners themselves got rich; in fact, many of them earned more in a week than a good teacher could earn in a year. It never seemed to occur to anybody that the sex instinct could reliably be depended upon to take care of itself, and that the calculus, on the other hand, couldn't."

"Sir," Jack said, "by 'popular music' do you mean music for dancing?"

"Oh, no," Langer said, "not in any sense you'd recognize. Of course, music for dancing has to be different from concert music in kind. But in those days it was vastly inferior in quality, too; in fact most of it was vile. And it was vile mainly because it was aimed at corrupting youngsters, and then after that job had been done, the corrupted tastes were allowed to govern public taste in music as a whole. We're very lucky that we ever got off that particular chute-the-chutes. It would never have unwound itself if it hadn't been for the revolution in education, which among other things involved the realization that music—and poetry— are primarily arts for adults, and for exceptional adults at that. The stuff that was being peddled to young people was all aimed at exploiting their inexperience in man-woman relationships; the producers knew that their targets weren't very well equipped by experience—and experience is the *only* teacher in that realm—to tell false coin from true, and that there was a lot of money to be made by exploiting them. And nothing could be done about it."

"Nothing at all?" Jack said.

"No, not at the time. It was already an age that suffered badly from censorship, which is in itself a crime against the mind. They couldn't suppress the trash without putting the same weapon in the hands of people who would have used it against masterpieces. The answer, as they gradually came to realize, was to fortify the minds of youngsters against trash—in short, the educational revolution. The celibate rule of the various cadet corps, of which Jerry's complaining, is only one outcome among many of that revolution."

"I wasn't complaining, exactly," Sandbag said. Nevertheless, Jack had the impression that Sandbag was not as impressed by Langer's reasoning as the trouble shooter obviously had intended that he should be.

"I should think," Jack said tentatively, "that they might have ruled that the bad stuff was a form of dope."

"Who'd have the power to make such a ruling, Jack? 'I like Bach, you like Hindemith, he likes Fritz Loewe; I have good taste, you are misled, he is a fool.' What would happen to the other two guys if the third were given the power to legislate over taste? For that matter, the very worst way to deal with dope itself is to make the traffic in it a crime. Addiction is a sickness; if you make it a crime, you can't get the victims to submit to treatment, and you run up the price on the stuff until it becomes so profitable to deal in it that some people are delighted to break the law to make their fortunes. The same goes for literature. Tell me, have you ever read any books with really wild sexual material in them?"

"A few. It gets kind of dull after a while."

"Precisely. But in those days, publishing that kind of thing was against the law—so an enormous amount of it was published, and commanded huge prices."

Jack scratched his head. "Dr. Langer, you make my grandparents sound kind of insane."

"They were insane," Langer said grimly.

For much of the rest of the time, Langer told stories mostly of past trouble-shooting jobs he had done for Secretary Hart. Many of them seemed as unfamiliar to Sandbag as they were to Jack; evidently Langer had been too busy during most of Sandbag's cadethood to indulge in much yarn spinning.

He was an excellent raconteur—not much to Jack's surprise—though inclined to be a little brief and telegraphic about the most colorful parts of the stories, particularly in explaining what he himself had done to unscramble the problem involved. Surprisingly, however, the stories were virtually free of violence. All of the magazine fiction Jack had devoured as a boy had pictured the ambassador from Earth pulling a gun in the clinches and holding off ravening hordes of aliens until help arrived, or great fleets of spaceships meeting between the stars in spectacular wars, or such stratagems as abductions, threats of assassination or encouraging revolt among the downtrodden masses. He said so, rather tentatively.

"Utter nonsense." Langer said at once. "I've lectured you both too much already, so I'll use only one example. Warfare will do. It is extinct—or we hope it is. A battle between two fleets of spaceships is a ballistic impossibility; there's no chance that they could intercept each other, or fight any sort of battle if they met by chance. A war between two planets would consist simply of one fleet wholly destroying its enemy's planet, while the other fleet was engaged in exactly the same errand. What would that solve? When you reach the age of space travel, and especially of interstellar travel, you realize that your home planet is only a grain of sand afloat in the middle of nothing at all. Any enemy you might get in a war with could wipe it out in twenty-four hours, and you could do the same to his home world—and neither of you could prevent the other from doing so. The essence of interstellar diplomacy is to make friends, not enemies. In the age of nuclear weapons, the only *real* enemy is war itself. All other differences between parties can be composed if you try hard enough; but once war breaks out, you've had it, on both sides. In diplomacy the first resort to force is a confession of failure."

"Suppose," Sandbag said, "we hit some planet sooner or later that doesn't agree?"

"Yes," Langer said, "that's the old problem of pacifism: How do you cope with a man who's perfectly willing to kill you to gain his own ends? But when both sides have nuclear weapons, as is necessarily the case in any conceivable interstellar war, that man has to bear in mind that his willingness to kill you also means committing suicide. That's a rather powerful generator of sober second thoughts."

"He could be crazy," Sandbag pointed out. "We were, a century ago. You said so yourself."

"True. There's no way around that risk. But I will tell you both a state secret. This is a test that we are going to have to pass. We are being watched to see whether or not we can pass it."

"Watched?" Jack said, stunned. "By the Angels?"

"No, the Angels can't have any interest in this problem; they seem to be immortal, or close to it. But we found out nearly a century ago that the four living intelligent races we know about in our limb of the Galaxy are all beginners, including our own. The whole center of the Milky Way is occupied by a huge confederation of peoples which has been stable and free of strife *for more than a million years* . . . despite the fact that their suns average less than a light-year apart, instead of the four light-years which is the average in our part of space."

Even Sandbag's garrulity was stifled by this revelation. "How do we know?" he whispered.

"They have observer satellites in our system, put there sometime in our Neolithic Age, about ten thousand years ago. We got signals from one of them way back in 1935, but didn't recognize them for what they were. The closest one to Earth is Phobos, the inner satellite of Mars; that was discovered on the third Martian expedition. It had been there when the Martians committed suicide. They are waiting to see if we do the same. They are not interested in unstable races."

Jack meant to whistle, but his mouth was too dry.

"How long do they give us?" he said. "I mean, how long do we have to last before they decide we're stable?"

40

"One hundred thousand years," Langer said. "We have about ninety thousand of those still to get through. And every new encounter with an alien people, like this with the Angels, could flunk us out.

"So you see, gentlemen, that you are not the only cadets aboard the *Ariadne*—or on the Earth. We are all cadets—the whole human race. And we cannot afford to flunk."

A day later, considerably sobered, they took their posts for the landing on Aaa. It would be their only stopover before the Coal Sack.

ENCOUNTER ON AAA   5

JACK WOULD HAVE liked to have seen a great deal more of the world of Aaa than the urgency of their mission would allow. It was a big place—a good 10,000 miles in diameter, though due to the fact that it had been short-changed when the metals were being passed out among the planets of its system, its gravity was almost exactly that of the Earth's. It had virtually no axial tilt, and as a result its climate was almost uniformly springlike, becoming chilly enough to snow only at the poles and even there only infrequently. And it was exceedingly verdant.

Whether or not it was also inhabited was another question, largely one of definition. It harbored a medium-sized, rather catlike creature with enough of a spoken language to have a name for its world, brains complex enough to fascinate the anatomists, and enough co-operativeness to have organized most of the planet. But on the other hand, the creatures had no hands capable of using tools—only rather ordinary animal paws—and did not make anything, not even shelters; nor could the xenologists rightly claim to have discovered among them anything that might be called a "culture." The situation in some ways resembled that of the bottle-nosed dolphin or porpoise on Earth, which had been found to be a sentient reasoning being of somewhat greater potential intelligence than man, but had yet to be surprised at doing anything with its formidable brains except playing complicated games.

For the time being, however, the Aaa were no problem, since Earth had no immediate plans to colonize the planet. It served only as a way station, which supported one semimilitarized base large enough to handle the traffic, and that was all—except for some tourists, for Aaa was a singularly beautiful planet to visit if you had the small fortune necessary to get there as a private citizen. The natives, if that was what they were, showed a tendency to shun human beings which was catlike indeed, and the laws against their being molested were strict and firmly enforced.

Sylvia McCrary, it swiftly developed, had the necessary small fortune—or an adequate equivalent.

Jack first encountered her in the lobby of the spaceport Administration Building. Langer had already gone off to the field commandant's office to complete his arrangements for supplies, repost his flight plan, and pick up any new orders that might have come from Secretary Hart while they had been traveling on the Standing Wave. Since they would be standing watches when they went into space again, Sandbag, who had the first trick, had been ordered below to snooze; this left Jack with a little freedom to look over the planet, or whatever of it he could manage to see without straying out of range of a summons from the trouble shooter.

He was delighted with the chance, for to him being on Aaa was just as much a part of being "in space" as spaceflight itself had been: a chance to touch an alien soil, to be shone upon by an alien sun, and just perhaps—though he really expected no such luck—to see an alien being. The brief description of Aaa in the ship's ephemeris was no more satisfying than seeing the planet on the *Ariadne*'s telescreens; he wanted to really *be* there, not just to be told he was there.

Seeing Sylvia was a shock. It was followed immediately by another: the realization that the blond man with his back to Jack, to whom Sylvia was talking animatedly, was none other than Sandbag.

Sylvia recognized him and waved enthusiastically. Sandbag turned, managing to look both guilty and defiant at the same time.

"Isn't this great?" Sylvia said the moment he joined them. "Your Dr. Langer isn't so invincible after all. I even got here ahead of you—imagine beating the *Ariadne*—and I even started after you did!"

That was another stunner; yet it was obviously true.

"How in the universe did you manage that?" Jack said, his curiosity overcoming him.

"I got Trans-Stellar to squirt me here in a proxy."

"I still can't get over that," Sandbag said. "You wouldn't get me into one of those things in a million years."

With this Jack concurred, two hundred per cent. A proxy was a press version of a Navy vessel—the Navy called them "drones"—which consisted of very little more than a hull, an ultra-hot drive and a television eye. Its purpose was simply to get to the scene of action ahead of any possible manned vessel and report back what was going on. It carried no crew, not even a pilot, its flight being guided by tapes. One out of every four of them was lost after launching, presumably having run into some situation which the tape didn't cover; but that cost was written off as one of the risks of getting fast coverage, or fast police information.

To ride in one as a passenger was outright foolhardly. It had of course been done a number of times before, but usually only in an extreme emergency—mostly, a medical emergency, requiring drugs and a doctor far sooner than any other kind of crash transport could get them on scene. Jack could think of only one occasion when Trans-Stellar had thought a story worth risking a reporter's riding a proxy, and then it had been one of their veterans, with a lifetime's background of taking such risks . . . not a girl with a brand-new competence ticket.

Furthermore, they had lost him.

He could think of nothing to say, but evidently his expression was readable. "And that's not all," Sandbag said. "Tell him, Sylvia."

"Trans-Stellar got me a temporary ticket as a historian-photographer," she said. "It's good for the Angels situation only, but for that it's good as gold. With that, I went back to Secretary Hart's office and got myself put on as recorder for the expedition—your expedition. So Langer or no Langer, I'm in— and I'm not only in, but I'm in three different ways at once."

"I doubt it," Jack said, but without much conviction. She really had covered herself on all sides with great ingenuity, to say nothing of a good many ingots of purest brass. She might well be a great reporter some day, if only she lived through throwing herself into risks like riding a probe. "But it isn't up to me to say. One thing, though, Sandbag. Dr. Langer put you on the next watch. If we run into any trouble, you'll wish you'd had your sleep."

"I'm not sleepy, Mr. Loftus," Sandbag said stiffly. "And my off-watch time is my own."

"Darn it, Sandbag, I know that. But you know how touchy

Langer is about slow reflexes on the drills. And if it all of a sudden *isn't* a drill, a quarter-second delay might make all the difference."

"I'm fast enough," Sandbag said. "Still faster than you are, I believe."

"I know," Jack said, "but it isn't a contest. It's a matter of everybody being as fast as he possibly can. And you've only got about four hours of shut-eye left, now. I don't like the idea of trying to get my own sleep knowing that my life's in the hands of a dopey watch officer."

"Oh, all right," the other said sullenly. "If you're scared, that's another matter. Good luck, Sylvia."

"Thanks, Sandbag." She watched him go. "Jack, don't you think you're being just the littlest bit too spit-and-polish about all this?"

"I'm only a cadet," he reminded her, "and so is Sandbag. Nobody trusts our judgment until we get our tickets. Until then we're supposed to stick to the regs like glue. You don't do Sandbag any favor by keeping him out of his bunk when he's due for the next watch."

"Why *Mister* Loftus, I do believe you're jealous."

This was getting worse and worse, but there was now no way out of it but straight through. "Langer picked me to do a job, and I'm going to see that it gets done, the best way I know how. If I have to bend over backwards to do it, I'll make myself look pretty comical, but all the same that's what I'll do." Suddenly he remembered Langer's revelation of the million-year-old galactic federation, and added: "And the stakes are a whale of a lot bigger than they look."

"I'll have you know that I'm here to do a job just as much as you are," the girl said hotly, "and I'm earning my own way, too. And as far as the stakes go, I know what they are—I knew about Lucifer long before you did."

"That's not what I meant," Jack said; but it was the wrong thing to say, for he could not tell Sylvia what he did mean—Langer had tagged the information secret. "I have to go. I've got things to do before my own sack time comes up—and I need my sleep, even if Sandbag doesn't."

"Nobody's keeping you here," Sylvia pointed out. "Sweet dreams, Cadet Loftus."

He strode back to the *Ariadne* in something closely approaching a fury. He was still fuming by the time he was seated on his own bunk, pulling off his boots. The whole encounter had been a disaster. He could think of a dozen things he should have said but didn't; and as for what he *had* said, he was prepared to believe that he would just as soon wipe it off the record, clean. And he was supposed to be in training as a diplomat!

Sweet dreams, is it? One boot hit the floor, hard. *What a sweet type she turned out to be!* The other boot followed. *If she doesn't make it as a reporter, maybe somebody will hire her on to sour cream.* What did Sandbag see in her, anyhow?

And he never had gotten a decent look at Aaa. All he had seen was a spaceport, very much like any other except for the oddly orange sunlight and the distant lining of green things that were obviously not trees.

And then the buzzer at the head of his bunk sounded. Resignedly, he began drawing the boots back on again. Langer wanted him, up forward.

This was going to be rough.

It was in fact even rougher than he had anticipated. Langer did not give either of them any quarter.

"Your off-watch time is *not* your own when it's covered by a direct order from me, any more than a green light lets you go when a cop's telling you to stop," he told Sandbag frostily. "In addition, as her complaint reads, your conversation with Miss McCrary appears to acquiesce to the status she aspires to on a number of points, and puts us in a tricky legal situation which cost me a lot of wasted time to straighten out. There are still a few knots in it about which I could do nothing from here. This is going to cost you quite a few months on your ticket, Jerry."

"Yes, sir," Sandbag said, white-lipped.

"As for you, Jack, you are technically in the clear, since you disobeyed no orders. But your handling of the situation as you hit it was overcautious, inflexible, and low on imagination—just the opposite of what I complain of in Jerry. You had better learn to play by ear a great deal better, or you'll wind up a desk officer at best. It's not up to me to penalize you, but I doubt that Secretary Hart will admire this performance any more than I do."

"Yes, sir," Jack said miserably.

Langer fell silent, but he did not dismiss them. For a while he simply sat and thought, once more looking a little plump and thoroughly harmless—except for his eyes. At last he said:

"Very well. Now we confront Sylvia. This mess is largely her doing; I can't blame either of you for her part in it. Especially since you're not the only victims. She sucked Tim Bearing into her net, too."

Despite himself, Jack released a croak of astonishment.

"I know how you feel, Jack. Tim is even more of a formalist about the regs than you are, though in his position it suits him better. But evidently Hart was out of the office when Sylvia showed up with her historian-photographer's ticket, and persuaded Tim that this also entitled her to that Department cachet as recorder for the expedition. Tim couldn't find anything in the rules against it, I suppose; or, more likely, he was even more rushed than usual and didn't have time to make a proper search of the rules, for there are a couple of clear precedents against it. Anyhow, he issued it to her. And that makes her responsible for three very large gray smudges on the records of three unusually able cadets."

Sandbag brightened visibly.

"Stow that," Langer said sharply. "Nobody doubts your ability, Jerry, or you wouldn't be here. Your judgment, however, is no better in my eyes than it was two minutes ago."

"Yes, sir."

"But what did you do, sir?" Jack ventured.

"I took refuge in the probable illegality of the cachet. It was all I could do on short notice. I also told her that I already had two pups to cope with and didn't want to take on a third even if I had room for her; and that in view of the way she had marred your records, and Tim's, she had better go home before she did more serious damage."

Sandbag suppressed a grin barely in time.

"Well, it *was* funny, but we haven't heard the last of it. Her parting shot was, 'My father was right after all.' What she means by that, I haven't the least idea, but I don't at all like the sound of it."

"Sir—" Jack said.

"Go ahead. Rest, gentlemen; the riot act is over. Just bear in mind that I meant it. If you have any comments, I'd welcome them."

Jack relaxed, though, not entirely, with a grateful sigh.

"Sir, I don't know what she means either, but I have a few notions. Wasn't it Shakespeare who said that hell hath no fury like a woman scorned? And when that woman is also a reporter for Earth's largest press association—"

"Yes; she could do a lot of damage," Langer agreed gravely. "There's where I wish Tim Bearing had told her a couple of great fat lies, instead of sticking so closely to the book. He could have saved us a lot of trouble. But that, of course, is why Tim is a cadet."

Jack frowned. He tried to follow Langer's logic, but there seemd to be no connection between the two lines of thought. "He's a cadet because he didn't lie to her?"

"Yes, Jack. As the Secretary remarked when he was discussing Lucifer, no intelligent being can afford to tell the truth all the time. Yet we do try to teach youngsters that honesty is the best policy, and mostly it is—especially when it comes to evading laws and regulations rather than meeting them squarely. Knowing when to tell a lie is almost as complicated an art as composing a wholly successful opera; you can't approach it without both talent *and* experience. So we have the cadet system—again it comes back to education—which makes young people defer to adult judgment no matter how skillful they are. Put it this way: If you are skillful, you can teach the left hand not to recognize what the right hand does; but this involves cutting the two hemispheres of the brain off from contact with each other. Both hands, and both hemispheres, must know what is going on, and participate in the act of judgement. If they don't, the result is paralysis. Here, let me show you a trinket I carry."

He went to the oversize locker and reached into his kit. When he came back, he was carrying a teaspoon. Its bowl was bent at right angles to its handle.

"This simple little thing is an instrument of torture, invented in the nineteenth century," he said. "It is, believe it or not, a right-handed teaspoon, impossible to use in the left hand. It was designed to force left-handed children to eat with their right hands."

"But why?" Sandbag said.

"Because left-handers are relatively rare, and their parents wanted to make them conform," Langer said, with disgust. "Mostly, they didn't succeed in switching the kids over to the right hand, although they tried very hard. But when they *did* succeed, can you guess what happened to the successes?"

"They turned out to be bad liars," Sandbag said, to Jack's amazed delight.

"Almost, Jerry; in fact I'll give you full marks for that one. But the actual outcome was worse. They turned out, in pitiful fact, to be incurable stutterers."

It was at that moment, for the first time in his life, that Jack saw the kind of concept which makes poetry differ from all the other arts. It seemed to be a perfectly useless sort of insight in his world of techniques and expedients; yet it filled him with an odd sort of warmth which he suspected he would cherish for many years to come. He tucked it away in his head, for later examination.

"But Tim didn't think fast enough to deal with Sylvia on that basis," Langer added, returning with almost a neck-snapping logical turn to the center of the subject. "And she probably knew him well enough to guess in advance that he wouldn't. The question in my mind is, why didn't her father stop her? A little earlier, he put on a great show of trying to."

"Weren't his hands tied after Tim gave her the cachet?" Jack said puzzledly.

"Not at all. Trans-Stellar Press is owned by a holding company which is also heavily represented on the board of directors of the corporation to which McCrary Engineering belongs. It's not officially a part of the four-company complex of that corporation, but all the same it's there—one of those situations that developed when major investors discovered that a thing called 'diversification' was almost an open road around the antitrust laws."

"Now I'm lost again," Sandbag confessed.

"What I mean, Jerry, is that if Paul X. McCrary had ever *really* wanted to block Sylvia from making a nuisance of herself to us, he could easily have found the means to do so. But he didn't. And I no more know why he didn't than you do. All I can say is that it doesn't make me feel any better about the way things are going."

Langer looked at each of them in turn, but neither cadet could find anything to add. He smiled ruefully.

"I sympathize. We'll just have to go on as before, and hope that once we're off Aaa we'll be able to deal with the *real* problem: the Angels.

"So: Posts. Up ship."

THE COAL SACK

AND NOW THEY were really cut loose from all contact with the Earth and its colonies, not only by being back on the Standing Wave, but in their deeper and deeper penetration of an area that had never been explored except by the disaster-ridden McCrary Fleet. Day after day the *Ariadne* hummed gently, almost inaudibly, and went light-years farther into the utterly unknown.

Twice the autopilot pinged to say that the *Ariadne* was passing within tempting distance of a new and promising planetary system, and twice Langer punched the RECORD stud to transfer the data to the log. They had no time for side jaunts now, and besides that was not what they were supposed to be doing. The new systems would have to wait for some other, less urgent expedition.

Nevertheless it gave Jack a twinge to have to bypass them. He would never know, except third-hand, what wonders they might conceal—wonders that he might have seen firsthand, and for the first time. Suppose that one of them harbored a truly intelligent race of a new and different kind . . . or even another mechanized observation post of the galactic federation itself? These were only daydreams, of course, but they were hard to put out of the mind, especially as the two marked solar systems dwindled and faded back into the welter of stars the *Ariadne* was leaving behind.

But ahead of them, the Coal Sack was growing.

It still seemed to be ahead of them long after they were actually in it, for the scattering of the dust particles in its outer reaches was far more tenuous than the hardest vacuum ever produced on Earth. Only its great size and the fact that it did contain more matter than ordinary interstellar space gave it its familiar appearance, even to the naked eye on Earth, of being a totally black hole in the Milky Way.

Its center still gave that appearance, for there the density of the nebula rose rapidly—fast enough, in fact, so that scientists believed new stars were being formed in its heart. And after a while, Jack began to notice that there were some visible aspects of the space around the *Ariadne* which were subtly different from what he had come to accept as normal.

For one thing, there seemed to be fewer stars, not only in front of them, where there were apparently almost none, but all around them, even to the rear. Furthermore, without exception, the fainter they were, the redder they were. This reddening puzzled Jack completely until he realized that what he was seeing was the scattering of the shorter wave lengths of light by the dust particles, the same phenomenon that reddened the sun and moon when they were on the horizon back home.

The instruments, of course, had been registering their entry into the cloud long before it could have been detected by human senses; in fact Langer had twice had to step them down in sensitivity to keep them from being saturated, at which point they would deliver no readings at all. There were storms going on out there in that near vacuum: torrents of free electrons, blasts of cosmic rays, great slow swirlings of the gas-and-dust medium itself. The detectors began also to notice the passage of meteors, ordinarily nearly nonexistent except inside a solar system, but here becoming more and more frequent by the minute.

And still the Coal Sack seemed to retreat ahead of them, spreading across the sky imperceptibly, like a mountain whose distance and size you have underestimated. Langer had the *Ariadne* down to a virtual crawl now, but though she was going well under the speed of light, he kept her on the Standing Wave.

"I don't know whether it'll do any good or not," he told them, "but a ship on the Standing Wave isn't detectable by any means that's known to us, and I'm hoping the Angels won't be able to do it either. Of course I'll have to take us into normal space when we adopt an orbit."

"Haven't seen any Angels yet," Sandbag said soberly. His tone was an odd mixture of disappointment and relief.

"No, I don't think there's enough available energy out this far to keep them comfortable. Of course they can travel outside the cloud completely, but I suppose they get pretty hungry after a couple of hundred years of that."

This reminder of the literally superhuman powers and

longevity of the creatures they were seeking did not serve to reassure Jack any.

"In fact," Langer went on, "I think we'll pull up now. We're not far from the perimeter inside which the McCrary Fleet ran into trouble, and I don't want to risk having my engines disabled by Angels, even friendly ones. We're about as far away as Neptune is from the sun from a suitable star—you can't see it because of the dust, but the tape shows it—and we'll just orbit around that for a while."

Jack started to ask a question, then thought better of it; but Langer had caught him at it.

"I know, Jack: How are we going to negotiate with the Angels if we try to hide from them? But I'm not going to hide, myself; I just hope to hide the *Ariadne*. We'll go on into the Coal Sack from here, but in a more suitable vessel."

Both cadets were properly baffled. Langer grinned.

"It's what's in the long, fore-and-aft locker. I can't really blame you for not having guessed, for to my knowledge such a thing has been used only once before in history. It's a photon-skiff—an interstellar sailing vessel."

"*Sailing?*" Sandbag said incredulously.

"That's right. It's very light in weight—really just a keel with a couple of lugs on it to hook our spacesuits to. Then there's a mile-long steel cable with a little atomic reactor at the far end, which is inertia-controlled to keep the cable rigidly at right angles to the keel at all times. On that cable we string up a mile-square sail of zirconium foil, which we rig with other small reaction motors by radio control. The radio impulses are pulse-modulated so that we don't pick up any static from the Sack."

Slowly, Jack managed to grasp the concept. Langer had designed his bizarre vessel to use the dust squalls, radiation storms and other disturbances raging invisibly in the Coal Sack. His sail would also respond to light pressure; in fact, since it was zirconium, it would even stop slow neutrons. But he thought he saw a flaw.

"That's going to be awfully slow, isn't it?" he said. "It seems to me it would take you half a century to go half a mile on a thing like that."

"It will be very slow at first," Langer agreed. "We'll have to start with just the *Ariadne*'s present orbital velocity, and when we push off we'll seem to you to be leaving at a velocity of only feet per second. But you'll be astonished at how fast light-pressure alone would build up the acceleration in normal space. In the Coal Sack, there is of course a great deal more energy for the taking. And since the machine has no driving engines, presumably it won't be as tempting to our fireplace-loving friends as the *Ariadne* would be."

"Sounds like a pretty wild way to travel," Jack said. "Uh, sir . . . you say I'll see you push off. I gather I'm not going along?"

"I'm afraid not, Jack," Langer said gently. "I'm sorry, but somebody has to stick with the ship. There are still important chores to be done here while we're gone. Jerry and I will sail the skiff in, and attempt to land on one of the barren nest-worlds the McCrary captain reported, to parlay with the Angels. We need you to stay here to bring the *Ariadne* in after us, because it won't be many weeks before all the junk that's flying around out there—I mean the solid stuff, not the charged particles—will have torn our sail to the point of uselessness."

"I see," Jack said; but he was bitterly disappointed.

"Jack, try to bear in mind that I'm trusting you with my ship," Langer added quietly. "There are very few people in the world who have been so privileged. And another thing: While you're waiting, you'll need to try to raise a signal from the disabled McCrary vessel, or otherwise find out where she is. You're going to have to do it in some way that will prevent the Angels in turn from getting a fix on the *Ariadne*. I haven't the faintest notion how you could go about it, but some way has to be figured out. I promised McCrary."

"Yes, sir. I'll come up with something."

"I'm sure of it. All right, Jerry, let's crack the suit lockers."

When the spacesuits came out, Jack was at first startled to find that their extra size was wholly accounted for by a huge hump on the back of each. He had expected them to be larger over-all, by reason of thicker shielding. When he examined the hump, however, while helping Sandbag into his suit, he realized where he had gone astray. It contained a small "fishbowl" type fission reactor whose output indicator was calibrated in Gauss units. In operation, it would surround the suit with a hard-driven magnetic field.

The chief radiation hazard Langer and Sandbag would encounter out here took the form of cosmic ray primaries: the stripped nuclei of iron and other heavy atoms, traveling at enormous velocities. Not only was material shielding useless against these—for they would go through sixteen feet of lead like so much tissue paper—but worse than useless, for the impact of the particle against the shield would produce a blast of secondary X-rays *inside the suit*.

The necessity, obviously, was to prevent them from hitting the suit at all. This was the purpose of the magnetic field. It would not fend them all off by any means, but those that did get through would have lost much of their steam, and furthermore would be traveling in arcs rather than straight as a bullet. That they would damage any body cells they hit was a certainty, but the magnetic field would probably keep the number of such hits below the critical level.

For a while. It was far better not to risk exposure at all, unless you had no choice. Ninety-nine per cent of the time you would not be conscious of the damage the impacts did, or the changes in your heredity that they sometimes made; but if one happened to hit a pain nerve, you felt it, all right—and even one such impact on the retina of the eye was a serious matter.

And this was far from the only mortal risk Langer and Sandbag were going to be taking. The chances were very high that he would never see either of them again.

The clumsiness of the redesigned suits, and the cramped quarters of the rebuilt control cabin, made it impossible to put them on except one man at a time in the well. Langer was already passing through the airlock while Jack was dogging down the last bolts on Sandbag's suit. Briefly he wondered if the fission reactors might not in themselves prove attractive "fireplaces" to the Angels, then dismissed the notion. They were relatively just match flames compared to a fusion pile.

Then Sandbag, too, was in the airlock, and Jack had the *Ariadne* to himself. It made him feel decidedly forlorn.

The radio on the board came to life. "This way, Jerry," Langer's voice said. "Jack, one other thing: Don't under any circumstances bring the ship in after us until you hear from us that it's safe to do so. Got that?"

"Yes, sir."

He adjusted one of the outside television eyes until he could look along the hull of the *Ariadne*. Langer and Sandbag, sliding along the ship's skin with the ice skater's shuffle made necessary by magnetic shoes, had already gotten the fore-and-aft locker open, and were lifting out the photon-skiff. From here it looked like nothing more than a thirty-foot-long steel I-beam.

The locker closed. The sound was clearly audible inside the ship.

"Jerry, go to the rear there and lock yourself onto the lug

53

you'll find there, by the waist of your suit. I'll do the same up front. . . . Are you secure?"

"Never felt more insecure in my life," Sandbag said. "But I'm locked on."

"Okay. Set your suit jets for two seconds' firing time at exactly. . . let me see . . . 1445. That's fourteen-forty-five, about three minutes from now. Got it?"

"Two seconds at fourteen-forty-five. Done."

"Shoes off."

They were now no longer magnetically locked to the *Ariadne;* but since they shared her velocity exactly, they stayed with her. Since her orbit was curved and they were now traveling in a straight line, they were actually drifting away from her; but the curvature was so vast it might take a week to put an inch of distance between their feet and the ship.

"Jack, hold the fort, and good luck," Langer's voice said briskly.

"Yes, sir . . . thanks. And—good hunting. So long Sandbag."

"Cheers," Sandbag said. But he did not sound at all cheerful.

The suit jets fired and the two spacesuits rose slowly, carrying the I-beam with them. Two seconds of acceleration was enough to push them away with a good deal more speed than the "feet per second" Langer had mentioned; in fact, at the end of the thrust they looked to be receding at better than a mile a minute. They looked grotesquely like two fat metal witches riding a broomstick.

Then the cable lifted from the center of the I-beam and unreeled swiftly, like an impossibly long snake. As it snapped to its full length, the great shining sail unfolded like a flower from around it.

The skiff dwindled swiftly. It was no longer possible to distinguish any part of it but the sail, and that too was getting smaller and smaller. Jack switched to full magnification. With that, he could make out the two men for perhaps a minute more, but the skiff was plainly picking up speed—still negligibly from the point of view of interstellar flight, but fast enough to carry it out of sight range quickly, even through the light amplifier.

The sail shifted position slightly to some unseeable order from Langer; he was apparently tacking. The skiff tilted and went even faster. It looked, as Jack had predicted, like a wild way to travel.

And after only a little while, the Coal Sack had swallowed it up.

* * *

54

The next week went by in utter silence. Jack was totally on his own, cut off from all human contact. He kept as busy as possible, but all the same it was nerve-racking.

The major chore, of course, was to attempt to pick up a broadcast from the disabled McCrary ship without himself being detected. He quickly discovered that Langer probably had not just been trying to make the problem sound hard by his remark that he could think of no way to do it himself. There were only a few reasonably detection-proof methods to try, and they were so insensitive that Jack might easily miss a fairly strong signal; whereas the chances were better than good that the disabled vessel was not putting out a signal at all. Whatever the reason, these methods did not yield a single trace.

His resentment against Langer cooled quickly with the discovery that the trouble shooter had actually handed him a genuinely tough nut. What now? Well, when detection-proof methods fail, the next stop ought to be to try methods which carry small but real risks.

He resisted this for several days, painfully aware that the discovery of the *Ariadne* might well mean the death of them all, and worse than that, the failure of the mission. But the awful silence and isolation warred with his caution. After a while, furthermore, he had conceived a method of hunting for the derelict which looked temptingly promising: a series of radar bursts pre-timed on tape to mimic the random gusts of static which were constantly sweeping through the nebula, the timing derived from a table of random numbers. Only he could know that that particular sequence had had an artificial origin; but if he got back an echo showing the same timing, he would have his object—or at least, some kind of object. Well, he could tune for the ship, whose class he knew fairly well. Only a metal meteor of similar size, shape and mass would be likely to fool him then.

But still, there was the danger. Partly to keep himself occupied, he was exceedingly meticulous about working out the risk of detection statistically. The figures seemed to show that the probability of his being discovered by the Angels after a single exercise of this search method was very low, and would stay that way if he altered the timing of the bursts after each broadcast. The last equation said that p was less than 0.13, meaning that such a discovery would have a 13 per cent likelihood of having occurred by chance alone. The books all said that this was tantamount to absolute safety.

All right, then, forge ahead. It took him half a day more to record the tape; only then did he turn to setting up the equipment. He was almost ready to turn the switch when the bobbing of a needle caught his eye.

There was a small, intensely radiating body nearby. With his heart in his throat, Jack set the outside scanner going.

It didn't matter now. He had *already* been discovered.

A single Angel was drifting in a slow, narrowing spiral around the *Ariadne,* well within visual observation distance.

FIRST CONTACT 7

AFTERWARD HE NEVER remembered acting; his first responses must have been pure reflexes. The next thing he knew was that he was sitting in darkness except for the little lights on the boards and the glow of the vision screens. The *Ariadne*'s reactor had been shut down, and even the battery power had been cut on everything but the absolutely essential services, such as the heat exchanger and the air pumps.

The sudden drop in power flow in the ship seemed to slow the approach of the Angel; perhaps it was puzzled. But it did not quite halt.

Jack was frightened—as frightened as he had ever been in his life—but he could not help being fascinated as well. After all, this was the first of the creatures he had ever seen, despite the long time his life had been intimately interwoven with their destinies.

This one was a duller, more somber scarlet than he had expected, though its quality of glowing from within at the same time made it seem almost gemlike. Furthermore, it was comma-shaped, almost like a shrimp, a resemblance which its color heightened. All the ones he had seen in pictures had looked more like teardrops—or drops of blood.

The lightninglike interplay of changes in its internal structure was clearly visible, and almost hypnotic in quality. He was amazed that there had ever been the slightest question as to whether or not this thing was alive. You could see that it was.

Once more its approach seemed to slow—either that, or it had abandoned the spiral approach for a direct one. But it didn't seem to be growing any bigger. Jack flashed a quick look at the scintillation counter; the reading was steady. The Angel had definitely come to rest, relative to the *Ariadne*. While he watched, the comma gradually modified itself into a perfect sphere.

Now what?

Gradually Jack realized that the scarlet sphere was pulsating, intermittently but regularly. This pulsation didn't show on the scintillation counter, so it wasn't going on at the hard-radiation end of the spectrum, but it was unequivocal in the much longer wave lengths of visible light. Jack thought suddenly: *And longer still? Could I get it on the radio?*

He could. Expressed as sound, it came from the speaker as a series of two quick, short tones on the FM band, the second tone slightly lower in pitch than the first. There was a slight indefiniteness of pitch to both notes, however, which was vaguely, almost maddeningly familiar.

Then he had it. The blurring modulations were an attempt at inflection. The realization made the blurs take shape.

The Angel was sending: "Hello. . . . Hello. . . . Hello. . . ."

After the first moment of stunned astonishment, Jack found himself in an agony of indecision. Should he respond? There was no way to guess what he would be involving them all in—not only himself and his comrades, but the Earth, too—by the simple act of replying.

Yet this was what he had been sent here for. And he, Jack Loftus, had been particularly chosen because he was supposed to be skillful at diplomacy. There was no choice.

He had better be good at it this time—better than he had been, say, with Sylvia McCrary.

"Hello," he sent back on the same band. "Can you sharpen up your signal? It's fuzzy and hard to understand."

"Need practice," the answer came back promptly, but the words were already a little clearer. "Let us speak more. You are an egg with an Earth-flesh in it, is that true? Like those first, that took one of us away?"

Treading cautiously, Jack said: "That's right. Except that we didn't take your brother away, not by choice. It was an accident."

"Yes. So he tells us. He says he has pleasure at Earth, that it is a very alive time for him."

Even amid the tension, Jack was staggered. So the Angels could talk with each other over so enormous a distance, evidently without any time lag! *That* would set the scientists on

57

their ears—if relations with the Angels ever settled down enough to let them study it. It also accounted entirely for this one's fluency in the language, despite the aural fuzz which still surrounded each syllable.

"We sent you two messengers," Jack said. "Have you talked to them?"

"We are not aware of them. There is no other egg like you in our nest."

Now, how was he going to explain the photon-skiff to this creature? It didn't even seem to have Jack and the *Ariadne* very well separated in its mind as entities. Still, it must know from Lucifer that human beings and spaceships were different kinds of things, and in fact it had already referred to Jack as "an Earth-flesh."

He clawed his way grimly through the explanation, keeping it as simple as he could. There was a long silence. Well, he could hardly have expected anything else. The Angel spoke his language, but they were two vastly different orders of life; it was amazing that they had made this much progress.

"I am in doubt," the voice said at last. It was eerie to realize that there was really no voice at all, that the Angel was emitting the radio waves directly, and almost surely believed that Jack was "hearing" them directly, too. "This is not a kind of artifact which could live in the nest. Nor could it be heard out here, even if it has fallen on one of the worlds. There is too much noise, both our own noise and the natural kind. I am sure we know nothing of it."

Jack's heart sank. The Angel's phrases were vague, but all the same they could imply but one thing: that the daring invasion of the Coal Sack had failed.

It had failed, obviously, of its own success. Not only did it use too little energy to tempt the Angels to occupy it, but too little to bring it to their attention at all. If Langer had managed to land on any of the barren planets deep inside, he could never manage to get a signal through to Jack over the static. He had probably entered that in his calculations and arranged to send an impulse capable of overriding the random noise of the nebula, but had not been able to follow for the fact, if he had thought of it at all, that a nebula swarming with Angels would also be in a constantly fluctuating roar of their conversations with each other.

And it was of course impossible to guess where the skiff might have fallen—if Langer and Sandbag had not been killed in flight by some flying piece of debris. If they *had* landed, they were marooned, for no amount of radiation pressure would ever lift the skiff against the gravity of even a very small planet.

At the thought, Jack grabbed for his slide rule and ran a quick calculation. The result was to deepen his despair. Even supposing the two men to be alive and whole, they would have a lethal dose of cosmic radiation some time within the coming three weeks . . . and he had no idea of where to look for them, and they no way of telling him.

"Hello. . . . Hello. . . ."

"I'm still here," Jack said, his voice gray with grief.

"Yes. But you had stopped sending."

"I was thinking. Don't you ever do that?"

"We always do," the Angel said. "But why does it take you so long? Is it because you are matter?"

"I suppose so." At the moment, the subject was of less than no interest to him. In fact, he wished that the Angel would just go away and leave him alone.

It showed no signs of doing so. Furthermore, if Langer and Sandbag were truly lost, the mission was now wholly in Jack's hands. Numb with shock though he was, he had to keep trying.

"We came here to make an agreement with you," he began.

"With all of us?"

"Yes."

"Then you must talk to others. I am too young. I was born only four million of your years ago, in the place you call the Orion nebula. They do not let me speak for all."

The Orion nebula? That was an enormous long distance from here. "How did you get to the Coal Sack, then?"

"We can make that kind of crossing," the Angel said. "We are not born of each other as you are. We are born out of the same processes which create stars. As long as we can find another nest where those processes go on, we continue to live. Many of us were born when the universe was born, and so have made such trips many times, as the old nests burned out and new ones came into being elsewhere. I am about to make my second."

"Oh? What for? The Coal Sack seems far from burned out."

"They do not want me here because I am young and weak and do not have enough of the— Because I cannot manipulate the— Because—" There was a short pause. "My brother at Earth says you do not have any word for this."

That time lag, during which this creature had spoken to Lucifer hundreds of light-years away, had been about four seconds, Jack guessed. He suspected that it had been taken up entirely by the conversation between the two Angels, not by any real lag in reception.

Though it was too late now, Langer's suspicions of Lucifer seemed thoroughly proven. Had Lucifer even told them that he could communicate instantly with his fellows in the Coal Sack, the *Ariadne's* mission would have been unnecessary . . . and the lives of a likable, gifted cadet, and of one of the most brilliant and valuable men on Earth, need not have been lost. Yet the fallen Angel had never mentioned it. It was possible, of course, that he didn't know the Earthmen didn't know it; it would be as natural to him as swimming to a fish. But it was hard not to resent the omission bitterly, even if it had been done without malice.

And in *this* Angel, Jack had hit a specimen who seemed equally unreliable, if for different reasons. Obviously he was never going to know precisely why the energy-being wanted to leave the Coal Sack. Its language suggested that perhaps its peers regarded it as being the sissy on the block; or, worse, that it had been ostracized because it was physically crippled somehow.

"If you don't object," he said grimly, "I'm going to call you Hesperus."

"Why?"

"Well, because I can talk to you more easily if I give you a name I can handle." There was no point in attempting to go into mythology now. "The name is our word for an especially beautiful star."

"Then I accept and have pleasure. When do you go back to Earth?"

"I don't know. I have to try and find one of you to talk to—and find my friends, if I can. Why do you ask?"

"I will go with you," Hesperus said. "I want to be the next of our race to go and live on the hearths of the Earth."

"But . . . but I thought you were on your way to make your second crossing!" Jack said, aghast.

"Yes. But as I was going out, I smelled the food leaking from your egg. Making a crossing is a time of starvation. If I travel inside your egg it will be a much more alive time for me, and Earth will be more interesting than a new nest. Nests are all alike except for their ages."

Another guess of Langer's confirmed, but the knowledge was of no help here. Not only had Jack failed to contact any Angel

60

with whom he could negotiate, but he was going to be the next Earthman to bring home an invading Angel—whether he liked it or not.

Unless he could talk Hesperus out of it.

"I'm not going back to Earth," he said, as firmly as he could manage. He didn't know whether Hesperus could interpret voice tone or not, but he was taking no chances. "First I need help in finding one of your brothers who can speak for all."

"I can be of no help. These in this nest are no longer my brothers."

"Darn it, Hesperus, you aren't even trying! I have to conclude an agreement between your race and mine. That's what I was sent here for. They won't let me come home without it. And I'm not going to—to warm up my egg for anything except to go deeper into the nest. That's final."

"What is 'final'?" Hesperus said, from the pinnacle of his near-immortality.

"I mean that I mean what I say!"

There was no reply. Maybe the Angels always meant what they said; if so, Jack's last sentence had been just noise to Hesperus. He was, Jack noticed, moving again. This time the movement was a sort of pendulumlike swing, rather erratic in timing, accompanied by changes in color Jack could not possibly have described. Was Hesperus losing his temper, or at least his patience? There was just no way to tell.

Nor did it seem possible to explain his problems to Hesperus in any way that the Angel could comprehend; maybe an older Angel—older than four million years!—would be more receptive, but with this one he had achieved nothing but a complete impasse.

"Look, Hesperus," he said at last. "Let me put it this way. I can't leave my two friends here, the ones that went into the nest on the 'artifact.' And I have other friends, who came here on the first trip, in a much bigger egg. That egg has probably been . . . uh, damaged, hurt. I have to try to save it."

"I look," Hesperus replied instantly, in a tone Jack would have sworn was surprised. "I know of *that* egg. Everyone does."

"Do you know where it is?" Jack demanded intensely.

"Yes."

"Will you lead me to it?"

The pause which followed might have been no more than a tenth of a second long; but to Jack, who had already become accustomed to Hesperus' lightning-fast thinking time—though

61

wholly unable to match it himself—the wait seemed endless. At last Hesperus said:

"Will you take me to Earth with you?"

Jack clenched his teeth. Again, success and failure, all wrapped up in one package! Hesperus was no longer talking in terms of going back with Jack whether Jack agreed or not; the strayed young Angel had grasped the concept of making a treaty. But the price he was setting was frightening. Hesperus brought back to earth willy-nilly was one thing; Hesperus brought back voluntarily was quite another. That was one agreement that Jack had no authorization to make.

"All right, Hesperus," Jack said slowly. "You've bought yourself a deal. Lead on."

"I do not understand the words."

"I said that I would carry you to Earth if you will lead me to the damaged egg."

"I cannot."

"But you said you know where it is!" Jack said, his voice rising despite himself to something very like a shout of exasperation. His nerves were unraveling rapidly.

"I do, but I cannot lead you there. I would have to take you there. There is no other way."

"Take me how?"

"By entering into your egg," Hesperus said.

"No, sir. No deal. Absolutely not."

"Then we cannot go," Hesperus said, with the accumulated patience of four million years. "There is no other way."

It took a maddeningly long time to understand even what Hesperus was talking about, let alone to begin to work out the basis for a possible new agreement. A glimpse of the ship's calendar accounted for at least part of the difficulty: Jack had now been without sleep for twenty hours. Until now he had not realized that the conversation had gone on so long; but of course it had not even begun until the ship's day was better than thirteen hours old. He had spent that much time just working on his now useless detector system, before Hesperus had even shown up.

There didn't look to be much sleep visible in the near future, either. He'd be lucky if he even managed to eat; and come to think of it, he hadn't since noon. He got a stick of protein concentrate out of the No. 2 locker and bit into it without bothering to cook it. It was tough and salty, but tasted unexpectedly good all the same. Maybe that would help him think, at least a little.

Hesperus had all the advantage here. He fed on starlight—the whole spectrum of it—automatically and without noticing, all the time, unless he happened to be in an energy-poor region of space. He almost surely didn't need sleep, either; after all, if the cud-chewing animals of Earth can get along without sleep, it ought to be easy for an Angel.

But now the problem. Essentially, it lay in the fact that Hesperus had been telling the literal truth, as seemed to be his habit. He did know where McCrary's wreck was, but he could not lead Jack to it, because he had no conception of the art of navigation as a human being might understand it.

Hesperus *lived* in the sea of space. He could no more give Jack a set of coordinates for the lie of McCrary's derelict than a porpoise could give a set of coordinates to a submarine. In both cases, the Angel and the porpoise knew directly where the place was, while the men had to find it by deduction. There was no common intellectual meeting ground between a race that needed a navigation grid and one that didn't, when both were operating in the same medium. A porpoise trying to find his way to Vallejo over dry land would have been in the same difficulty, and a man, no matter how helpfully inclined, would have been hard put to it to explain a gas-station road map to him.

But it was perfectly possible for Hesperus to bring Jack to the derelict. All he needed to do was to enter the *Ariadne* and actuate her guidance circuits, using them in effect as though they were his nerves, and her drive his muscles (though he had neither). He would, in effect, become the brain of the *Ariadne,* displacing Jack as that organ; then he could "swim" her wherever he liked.

But he could not act as her pilot fish; nor would it be useful to play follow-the-leader in this situation. Keeping Hesperus in sight in that kind of game would be too slow. They needed the full speed of Langer's cruiser now—and could not have it without Hesperus effectively in control of her.

Was this risk worth taking? In one sense, at least, it was directly contrary to his express orders. He had been left aboard the *Ariadne* to preserve her from the Angels, if at all possible— not to hand her over to one of them.

On the other hand, Langer had envisioned no such situation as this—whereas Langer's own gambit had failed. If you want to

63

talk to the Angels, obviously you must expose yourself; otherwise they are incapable of noticing you. Hesperus himself had passed close enough to the *Ariadne* to detect her only by a huge coincidence.

Obviously, Jack hadn't the faintest chance of rescuing Langer and Sandbag—or anybody aboard the derelict McCrary ship *Probe,* presuming anybody aboard her was in any shape to be rescued—unless he now entered the heart of the Coal Sack. Nor did he have any chance of making it with the guidance, risky though it was, of Hesperus.

Jack gulped down the last of the protein concentrate and stared around the empty, still darkened control room. The glinting metal surfaces and the little lights gave him back no answer. He was on his own.

Well . . . he *was* supposed to negotiate. And he had even made a little progress: He had educated one Angel in the concept of negotiation, at least. But this one was obviously atypical, offering him no real clues which would enable him or the Earth he represented—all by himself, now—to win the kind of agreement that it was vital to have. Again, there was no hope for that except the chance of penetrating deeper into the nebula. All roads led back to Hesperus.

Was there anything on *his* side? Yes, there was. He had taught Hesperus the essence of making a deal. Hesperus was not waiting for permission, instead of simply taking over the *Ariadne,* as he had originally planned to do, and as he could still do if he wanted—

Or could he?

In fact, he couldn't. Jack had shut the Nernst generator off, and there was a good chance that it could stay off at least for a while. There was more than enough juice in the accumulators to drive the *Ariadne* a good distance before fusion power would be needed again. Hesperus could use that. The Nernst generator could continue to stay cold, especially if Jack disarmed the switch, so that Hesperus couldn't use his control of the *Ariadne's* "nerves" to get the generator started again. In fact, it would be a good idea to disarm that switch right now, just in case.

Quickly he pulled its fuses, and for safety's sake also squatted down under the boards and removed about three feet of lead line on each side of the switch. That would do it, for sure! Now he had a weapon—or at least, a carrot.

"Hello. . . . Hello. . . ."

"Wait, Hesperus, I'm still thinking."

What about it? All the logic he had been able to bring to bear on the question pointed in the same direction: into the Coal Sack.

And in addition to logic, there was intuition. This was a talent that Sandbag had had much more practice in developing than Jack had—but Sandbag was gone. Nevertheless, in the lonely control cabin of the *Ariadne*, Jack was sure he had a hunch; and the hunch was, that he understood Hesperus . . . at least a little bit. There was an elusive something about the four-million-year-old cadet Angel that reminded him of himself.

"Hesperus?"

"I hear."

"If I agree, I'm still not going to warm up the egg yet. Not until some time after we find the big egg, the damaged one. You'll have to make do with whatever other food you find here."

A faint, nonverbal sound. Disappointment? Maybe; maybe not; but at least, no outright rebellion.

"Very well, I do agree. Come aboard."

He never saw Hesperus move; the Angel simply vanished.

Seconds later, the *Ariadne* was in motion toward the black heart of the nebula.

A TEMPLE OF STARS 8

IT WAS A frustrating and alarming sensation to feel one's self being hurtled faster and faster into the unknown aboard a ship not even remotely under human control. Jack found time to wonder if Sylvia had felt anything like this, during her ride to Aaa aboard Trans-Stellar's proxy. Probably not, he decided (completely wrongly); Sylvia had too much brass to let anything like this scare her.

But it sure scared him.

The space outside the *Ariadne* became murkier and harder to see through with every minute. After a few hours there was nothing visible in the screens but a backdrop of soot, through which a very few nearby stars burned redly as they passed. This didn't seem to bother Hesperus in the least; he kept piling on the acceleration—and doing it in normal space, for either he hadn't yet discovered the Standing Wave drive or he didn't understand its function. Even at seven-tenths of the speed of light he was still relying on his fishlike style of ducking, dodging, twitching and reversing his field to avoid major chunks of matter. The minor ones he simply rammed into, if he "saw" them at all. Luckily, at this velocity the *Ariadne's* mass had gone up so enormously that such bubbles exploded into vapor before they could do much worse to her than etch her skin a little.

But it was very hard on Hesperus' passenger. He considered letting Hesperus in on the secret of the Standing Wave. Not only would it save Jack the severe battering he was getting, but it would also save time—and there were only three weeks left, after all, to find Langer and Sandbag, if they could be found at all. Even considering how closely spaced were the stars inside the cloud, three weeks at sub-light velocities would get the *Ariadne* essentially nowhere . . .

. . . Except that she had *already* passed three or four stars in the first day of flight!

Evidently he didn't need to worry about betraying the Haertal equations to the Angels. Whatever they had, it was better.

"Hesperus?"

"Receiving."

"How are you managing to chew up so much distance at less than the speed of light?"

"I will have to ask my brother on Earth for the words. . . . Yes. We are cruising a vector in normal space between the two time axes, *t*-time and *tau*-time. The distances covered are more or less real, but the times involved cancel out except for a loss due to . . . ? . . . Yes, Planck's Constant. The principle is much like the one that is used by this artifact in your egg, the . . . ? . . . The Haertel overdrive. But much simpler."

"Oh. But does it have to be so rough?"

"Rough? Oh, erratic. Yes, we are still in normal space, not isolated as your artifact would isolate us. I will attempt to smooth the turns somewhat."

Hesperus' idea of smoothing things out benefited Jack very little. He was finally driven to suiting up and immersing himself in the thick oil of the *Ariadne's* small anti-acceleration tank, from which he watched the scene outside the ship as best he could through the spacesuit's circumscribed orthicon goggles.

Even under these limitations, he began to spot other Angels with increasing frequency, and finally, several at a time. At this rate, he could expect to be seeing whole squadrons in another day or so.

Curiously, however, none of them paid any attention to the ship. Did they have some way of knowing that the *Ariadne* was already occupied by one of their number? Or were they simply ignoring her because her "fireplace" wasn't going? He wondered abruptly how much power Hesperus' version of the interstellar drive was draining out of the batteries; since he was no longer stationed at the boards, he had no way of checking the matter. He was anything but eager to discover that he might have to fire up the Nernst generator to make a getaway when the time came, this deep inside Angel territory. But there was nothing he could do about that from the middle of a tank of viscous oil—or out of it either, probably.

As they proceeded inward, the cloud paradoxically began to thin out and become brighter . . . why, he could not at first imagine, and his limited vision and lack of instruments provided him with few clues. At the same time, the course the *Ariadne* was following under Hesperus' control gradually lost its resemblance to the flight of a housefly inside a closet, until she was lurching no more than she might have in the hands of an unusually nervous human cadet. Evidently there were not so many heavy meteors and other material objects zipping and zooming about in this area, either.

"Earth-flesh."

"Darn it, my name is Jack."

"What does that mean?"

"I don't remember, if I ever knew. Use it anyhow."

"Very well, Jack," Hesperus said. "We are decelerating and the stresses will drop from now on. You might emerge from your inner egg if you so wish, without great danger. You get born very often in your short lives, I see."

Jack sputtered for a moment, and then subsided. It was a useful reminder that on many important subjects, he and Hesperus were as far from understanding each other as ever—and might never draw much closer. This creature could talk to him; but all the same, it was *alien*.

He went through the tank lock, got the oil steamed off his suit, and emerged cautiously into the well, where he shed the suit in turn. It was very hard to do without anybody to help him with the dogs at the back; with a teammate to assist, a spacesuit opens like a tired clam. But he got out of it somehow, and got it stowed in the lockers. The empty clamps which had held Langer's and

Sandbag's suits wrung his heart despite his exhaustion; he slammed the locker doors on them hastily and went to the boards.

The scene spread out before him in the screens was one of incredible and baffling magnificence. The suit goggles had not been able to accomodate enough of it even to hint at it; the very first sight of the whole made him gasp.

In the heart of the Coal Sack was a separate universe. It was a great shimmering cluster of newborn stars, so close together at the center as to make up one solid mass of blue-white fire . . . an illusion brought about by distance, but no less stunning for all that. Outside this treasure trove of heaped jewels, nothing could be seen at all, for the rest of the plenum was cut off by the curtaining storms of the Sack itself. Here, however, most of the gas and dust had been used up in creating these diadems of suns.

Not all of it, however, for streamers and feathers of it, sometimes dark against the general glitter and glare, sometimes flourescing in response to all this raw energy against the black backdrop of the Sack, wove in and out among the new stars. These wisps writhed actively even to the naked eye; creating was still taking place here, and the primal atoms were being driven in unthinkable herds around the birth-field to be taken unto the bosom of some star still forming. Their hurricane to-and-fro flight made a faint but audible whispering, like the wash of a tide, along the hull of the *Ariadne;* in the face of that onslaught, many of the more sensitive instruments had given up, most of them obviously blown out hours ago.

How big was this bubble of joyful fire? A hundred light years? A thousand? There was no way of telling, for the other side of it offered no landmarks to figure from, only that unvarying sooty backdrop of the inner edge of the Coal Sack. No wonder the Angels thought of their clouds as both egg and nest at once.

And as the *Ariadne* edged onward to the will of one of the natural creatures of this miracle, Jack began to see that not only natural forces were involved here. At first there were only a few disquieting traces of this; hints, nothing more, teasing at Jack's unpracticed intuition; but gradually, they began to change from hints into bits of evidence.

The new star cluster had a structure . . . an artificial structure. Though he could not put a name to it, Jack recognized it. It was related to those swift flickerings of organization, evanescent but visibly living, which he had watched going on inside Hesperus while he and the renegade Angel had been sparring with each

68

other. Those changes were taking place here, too, but much more slowly, as befitted the vastness of the heart of the nebula.

More: There was a hierarchy of such structures, becoming firmer, more definite and more complex as the *Ariadne* went deeper into the labyrinth following the thread that Hesperus had woven for her. At the very center, there could be nothing less than a cosmic temple, built from gas, dust, energy and stars to celebrate some mystery beyond the fathoming of so short-lived a creature as man.

Could it be, in fact, that the joke of naming these creatures "Angels" had not been a joke at all? Could it be that they had some direct role to play in the birth of new stars? Could it be that they had participated—at least the oldest of them—in the First Cause itself, the Cause which had given birth to the whole universe?

One answer was already in. The central temple of this great cluster was as alive as the Angels were, and in the same kind of way. Jack could not have defended his knowledge of that for an instant against a skeptic, but he knew it was so. He could see it. Anyone could see it!

But about this he was wrong. He never saw that central temple, if it exists; nor has anyone else seen it since. It may be alive, as Jack thought; or it may not. Howard Langer may have come a little closer to it, but if he did, he saw less of it than Jack did. The Angels guarded their mysterious heaven very closely, then as now; and the First Cause remains unplumbed.

"Jack," he started, and a little of the rapture dissolved. "Receiving, Hesperus."

"We are coming to rest. Your damaged egg is just ahead."

"Up there?" Jack whispered hoarsely. "In the—in the main star structure?"

"No. This is not the main structure. You cannot see that from here, it gives too much light. What you see is only a local nexus, only just built. Your egg is in the middle of it."

Jack dimmed the screen, trying to make sense of the flood of light pouring into the *Ariadne*. After a while his eyes had adapted enough to see what Hesperus had meant. This was only a sub-temple simply *because* its center was nearby, whereas all the structural clues indicated that the main pattern had to be in the center of the cluster. It was stunning enough in itself, but necessarily less grand than the whole of which it was a part.

After a while, too, he could see the lost *Probe*—and that one glance told him that nobody aboard her could be alive. The last third of her hull was shrunken and wrinkled where she had melted, which meant that her Nernst generator, though it had not exploded—there would be no ship at all if that had happened—had certainly run wild. And she was completely unsalvageable, even for scrap, for his instruments told him she was intensely hot, not only radioactive but in the ordinary kitchen-stove sense as well.

He doubted very much if he would have been allowed to tow her out even had she been relatively whole, moreover, for now she was a center of activity for the Angels—hundreds of them. They whirled and danced and swung around her in a maze of streaking curves and orbits, until she resembled nothing so much as an animated three-dimensional model of a uranium atom. It was impossible to figure out what all this action meant. It seemed to be part frolic, part ceremony, and part something else entirely beyond Jack's understanding.

Hesperus' voice said quietly: "We are being visited."

Jack started and looked first into the port view-screen, then into the starboard. Sure enough; coming toward them from the right was a band of Angels (the collective noun was wholly unavoidable)—five of them, cruising in a regular pentagon, its face presented to the *Ariadne*.

"The one who seems a deep orange to your senses belongs to the First-Born," Hesperus added. He sounded quite subdued, somehow. "The others were born in the Pleiades—very ancient, but not so ancient as he."

Was this, then, the moment? Once more catching a glimpse, out of the corner of his eye, of that vast play-plus-ritual-plus-X swirling around the derelict, he felt again the futility of hoping to negotiate with a race so remote from humanity as this one.

"He will speak with you," Hesperus said. "Henceforth I am forbidden."

"For good, Hesperus?"

Silence was his only answer. Under the circumstances, it seemed conclusive enough.

There couldn't very well be a worse beginning than this. He had been deprived of his only possible ally.

"Earth-flesh in the egg!"

"My name is Jack," he said, with the boldness of hopelessness. "And I will address you as Gabriel."

"Why?"

70

He had already learned to expect that question, and he had the answer ready. "Because it is my will."

"That is sufficient, Jack. And it is our will that you be thrust from our nursery." So *that* was what the missing "X" was— teaching! "The one you call Hesperus did a crime to bring you here, and for this he will be deprived of. . . . ? . . . There is no word. Because you did not know that this was a crime, we exact no penalty of you; but we will put you out, and it is forbidden that any of your race ever enter our nests again—this nest you call the Coal Sack, or any other birthplace of stars and people."

Jack had no taste for gambling; but if ever in his life he shook the dice, it was now.

"You are wrong, Gabriel," he declared, in a voice that he could not prevent from breaking a little. "It was Hesperus who was in the right. The damaged egg in the center of your nursery is my property and the property of my race, and it was proper of Hesperus to lead me to it. You in your turn have been responsible for the deaths of some hundreds of my race. Causing death must be the ultimate in horrible crimes for a race as long-lived as yours. Is this not true?"

"It is true."

"Yet we in turn do not charge you with this, because we know it was an accident; like you, we can be forgiving. But the egg is my property, and I'm not leaving without it."

CRISIS IN THE HEAVENS 9

JACK HAD NEVER had any reason to doubt Hesperus' early implication that the thinking processes of the Angels were almost instantaneous. Nevertheless it did not surprise him that his challenge to Gabriel produced a long silence. This was not, for the Angel, just a matter of running through a logical or deductive chain, or deciding on some action from some already established premise. No doubt the Angels could do that kind of thing as fast as any computer.

What Gabriel was being asked to do now, however, was to re-examine all his basic assumptions, make value-judgments on them, and give them new and different powers in his mind to govern his motives. This is not wholly a reasoning process—a computer cannot do it all—and even in an Angel it takes time. (Or, perhaps, *especially* in an Angel, whose assumptions had mostly been fixed millions of years ago.)

Being reasonably sure of the reason for the long pause, however, did not make it seem any less long to Jack. He had already become used to Hesperus' snapping back answers to questions almost before Jack could get them asked.

There was nothing he could do but wait. The dice were cast.

At last Gabriel spoke.

"We misjudged you," he said slowly. "We had concluded that no race as ephemeral as yours could have had time to develop a sense of justice. Of course we have before us the example of the great races at the galactic center; individually they are nearly as mortal as you—the difference does not seem very marked to us, where it exists. But they have survived for long periods *as races,* whereas you are young. We shall recommend to them that they shorten your trial period by half.

"For now, it is clear that we were in the wrong. You may reclaim your property, and the penalty on Hesperus is lifted. Hesperus, you may speak."

"I did not perceive this essential distinction either, First-Born," Hesperus said at once. "I was only practicing a concept that Jack taught me, called a deal."

"Nevertheless, you were its agent. Jack, what is the nature of this concept?"

"It's a kind of agreement in which each party gives something to the other," Jack said. "We regard it as fair only when each party feels that what he has received is as valuable, or more valuable, than what he has given." His heart, he discovered, was pounding. "For instance, Hesperus agreed to help me find my property, and I agreed to take him to Earth. Between individuals, this process is called bargaining. When it is done between races or nations, it is called making a treaty. And the major part of my mission to your nest is to make a treaty between your race and mine. Recovering the property was much less important."

"Strange," Gabriel said. "And apparently impossible. Though it might be that we would have much to give you, you have nothing to give us."

"Hesperus and Lucifer," Jack said, "show that we do."

Another pause, but this one was not nearly as long.

"Then it is a matter of pleasure; of curiosity; of a more alive time. Yes, those could be commodities under this concept. But you should understand, Jack, that Hesperus and Lucifer are not

72

long out of the nursery. Visiting the Earth would not be an offering of worth to those of us who are older."

This explained a great deal. "All the more reason, then," Jack said, "why we must have a treaty. We will gladly entertain your young and give them proper living quarters, in return for their help in running our fusion reactors. But we must know if this is in accordance with your customs, and must have your agreement they will not misuse the power we put in their hands, to our hurt."

"But this simply requires that they behave in accordance with the dictates of their own natures, and respect yours in turn. To this we of course agree."

Jack felt a wave of complete elation, but in a second it had vanished without a trace. What Gabriel was asking was that mankind forego all its parochial moral judgments, and contract to let the Angels serve on Earth as it is in Heaven *regardless* of the applicable Earth laws. The Angels in turn would exercise similar restraints in respect for the natural preferences and natures of the Earthmen—but they had no faintest notion of man's perverse habit of passing and enforcing laws which were contrary to his own preferences and violations of his nature.

The simple treaty principle that Gabriel was asking him to ratify, in short, was nothing less than total trust.

Nothing less would serve. And it might be, considering the uncomfortable custom the Angels had of thinking of everything in terms of absolutes, that the proposal of anything less might well amount instead to something like a declaration of war.

Furthermore, even the highly trained law clerk who was a part of Jack's total make-up could not understand how the principle could ever be codified. Almost the whole experience of mankind pointed toward suspicion, not trust, as the safest and sanest attitude toward all outsiders.

Yet there was some precedent for it. The history of disarmament agreements, for instance, had been unreassuringly dismal; but the United States and the Union of Soviet Socialist Republics nevertheless did eventually agree on an atomic bomb test ban, and a sort of provisional acceptance of each other's good intentions on this limited question. Out of that agreement, though not by any easy road, eventually emerged the present world hegemony of the United Nations; suspicion between member states still existed, but it was of about the same low order of virulence as the twentieth-century rivalry between Arizona and California over water supplies.

Besides, agreements "in principle," with the petty details to be thrashed out later, were commonplace in diplomatic history. The trouble with them was that they almost never worked, and in fact an agreement "in principle" historically turned out to be a sure sign that neither party really wanted the quarrel settled.

Suppose that this one were to work? There was no question in Jack's mind of the good faith on one side, at least. If mankind could be convinced of that . . .

It was worth trying. In fact, it had to be tried. It would be at once the most tentative and most final treaty that Earth had ever signed. Secretary Hart had taught Jack, at least partially, to be content with small beginnings in all diplomatic matters; but there was no small way to handle this one.

He turned back to the screens, the crucial, conclusive phrase on his lips. But he was too late. He had lost his audience.

For a moment he could make no sense at all of what he saw. It seemed to be only a riot of color, light and meaningless activity. Gradually, he realized that the pentagon of Angel elders had vanished, and that the ritual learning dance of the nursery had been broken up. The Angels in the nursery were zigzagging wildly in all directions, seemingly at random.

"Hesperus! What's going on here? What's happened?"

"Your brothers have been found. They are on their way here."

"Where? I don't see them. The instruments don't show them."

"You can't see them yet, Jack. They'll be in range in a short while."

Jack scanned the skies, the boards, and the skies again. Nothing. No—there was a tiny pip on the radar; and it was getting bigger rapidly. If that was the skiff, it was making unprecedented speed.

Then the skiff hove into sight, just a dot of light at first against the roiling blackness and crimson streaks of the Coal Sack. Through the telescope, Jack could see that both spacesuits were still attached to it. The sail was still unfurled, though there were a good many holes in it, as Langer had predicted would be the case by now.

It was a startling, almost numenous sight; but even more awesome was the fact that it was trailing an enormous comet's-tail of Angels.

The skiff was not heading for the nursery, however. It seemed unlikely that her crew, if either of them were alive, could even see the *Ariadne*, for they were passing her at a distance of nearly a light-year. And there would be no chance of signaling them—without the Nernst generator Jack could not send a call powerful enough to get through all the static, and by the time he could rebuild his fusion power the skiff would be gone.

Fuming, helpless, he watched them pass him. The sail, ragged though it was, still had enough surface to catch some of the ocean of power being poured out from the nursery stars. He would never have believed, without seeing it, that the bizarre little vessel could go so fast.

But where was it going? And why was it causing so much agitation among the Angels, and being followed by so many of them?

There was only one possible answer, but Jack's horrified mind refused to believe it until he had fed the radar plots of the skiff's course into the computer. The curve on the card the computer spat back at him couldn't be argued with, however.

The skiff was headed for the very center of the nebula—toward that place which, Jack knew now, could hold nothing less important than the very core of the Angel's life and religion.

It was clear that Langer had at last found a way to attract the Angels' attention.

It was equally clear that as of this moment, the treaty was off.

STERN CHASE   10

LANGER WOULD HAVE to be headed off, whether he knew where he was going or not. Almost surely he did; after all, he had had the same set of facts as Jack had had to work from, and he was an almost frighteningly observant man. But not having talked to the Angels, he had made a wrong turn in his reasoning somewhere along the line. Had he decided, perhaps, that the center of the cloud was a center of government, instead of a center of life and faith?

But it didn't matter now whether he meant to invade the Holy of Holies, or was simply headed in that direction by accident. If it was intentional, it was now also unnecessary; and whether intentional or not, the outcome would be disastrous.

Jack crawled under the boards and restored the six feet of lead line he had excised from the Nernst generator switch. When he was back on his feet again and about to reinstall the fuses, however, he hesitated.

He had to have fusion power to catch up with the skiff and he had to have it fast. But fusion power in the Coal Sack was what had triggered all the trouble in the first place—and he already had an Angel aboard.

"Hesperus?"

"Receiving."

"I'm going to turn my generator back on, as I promised to do. But I can't take you to Earth yet. First I've got to intercept my brothers before they get any deeper into trouble. Will you obstruct this, or will you help? I know it's not part of the bargain, and your elders might not like it."

"Nobody else can live in your hearth while I am in it," Hesperus said promptly. "As for my elders, they have already admitted that they were wrong. If because of this incident they become angry with Earth, I will not be permitted to go there at all. Therefore of course I will help."

With a short-lived sigh of relief, Jack plugged the fuses back in and threw the switch. Without an instant's transition, the green light that meant full fusion power winked on the board. Always before, it had taken five minutes to—

Of course. Hesperus was in there. From here on out, the *Ariadne* was going to be hotter than any space cruiser man had ever dreamed of.

But since he had failed to anticipate it, he lost the five minutes anyhow, in plotting an intercept orbit.

"Hesperus, don't use this *t-tau* vector trick of yours, please. I think we'll get into less trouble if we travel on the Standing Wave."

"Why? That is less efficient."

"Less efficient for you, but more efficient for me. I've got to be at the control boards, not in the acceleration tank. Besides— isn't it true that our elders can't detect us as long as we're on the Standing Wave?"

"Yes."

"Okay. Here we go."

The *Ariadne* darted away from the deserted nursery of the Angels like a salmon leaping a waterfall. At these velocities, Jack realized, the stern chase would not be very long, for the skiff when last seen had been making only a little over the speed of light in normal space—it would be nice to know how Langer had managed that trick, without any access to the Angel's method of doing it—under about eight gravities of acceleration. It could not have gotten very far away since then, at least as compared to the distance the *Ariadne* could have covered in the same amount of time.

The danger was not that Jack couldn't catch the skiff in a hurry, but instead that without the most precise control, he might easily overshoot it. What he had to do was draw abreast of it and match velocities, so that he could try to pull it aboard.

And that couldn't, after all, be done if he tried to do most of his cruising on the Haertel overdrive. Reluctantly, he strapped himself as tightly as he could into the seat before the left board—Langer's seat, when he was here.

"Hesperus, you were right. We'll have to do this the hard way. Take us off the Standing Wave and onto that time-differential drive of yours. But take it easy, will you?"

"Okay."

The flight was in fact a good deal less rough than before, but whether that was because Hesperus had accurately assessed Jack's weaknesses as a flesh-and-blood creature, or because he was forced to follow the course laid out by the computer with considerable fidelity, would be hard to say. Nor did it matter at the moment. Results were what counted.

Still, Jack was going to be cherishing quite a few strap bruises by the time he got out of this situation . . . if he got out of it at all.

Locating the skiff by eye proved to be relatively easy, for its comet's-tail of Angels became visible long before the skiff itself could be seen. He tried to put out a call to Langer, but nothing came back over the static, which was becoming steadily worse as they proceeded inward toward the center of the cluster.

Something prompted him to take a quick look at the rear viewscreen as well. Sure enough: he had his own comet's-tail now. The *Ariadne* and the skiff between them seemed to be being followed by virtually every Angel in the nest.

About which he could do exactly nothing at all. He did not even know what it meant, though his suspicions were black and disquieting. If the Angels were to step in and halt the skiff before the *Ariadne* could intercept it, or, still worse, stop the *Ariadne*, they would all be lost, mankind included.

Thus far, however, they were only following; for which he tried to be grateful.

Now the skiff itself was visible at highest magnification, as a

77

black point, almost swamped out against the flood of the glare from the center of the star cluster. Jack called for a brief burst of acceleration, and was rewarded by seeing the point turn into a tiny black square, like a beauty patch; the sail in silhouette. Once more he called upon every erg of available power to hail the fragile vessel and its doomed crew.

"Dr. Langer, Sandbag Stevens. This is Jack Loftus. Turn around. Put about. Urgent. Urgent. Put about. The *Ariadne* will pick you up. Dr. Langer, urgent, put about!"

Nothing came back from the speaker but a Niagara of stellar static.

"Hesperus, we're not close enough, and we're losing precious time. Can you run up the acceleration, back it down, and decelerate to bring us to rest with respect to the skiff, on an asymptotic curve? It's got to be that way or you'll crush me to death."

"I don't know what that is, Jack."

"The computer can tell you. Check it fast."

"All right," Hesperus said calmly. "I know what it is now. Hold on, and don't make any unnecessary movements."

The acceleration began to build, crushingly. Sweating, Jack clutched the microphone to his breast in both hands and croaked:

"Dr. Langer . . . Jack Loftus calling. Put about. Dr. Langer, urgent, put about . . . Urgent . . . urgent . . . Put about."

The skiff grew on the screen, but still there was no reply from the speaker—only the cataract of noise. The *Ariadne* went faster. The Nernst generator light had changed from green to yellow, and the air stank of ozone; Hesperus was giving the ship hard treatment. Jack only hoped that by now he knew her circuits well enough not to push them past the blow point.

"Calling Dr. Langer . . . Jack Loftus calling Langer or Stevens. Urgent . . . Urgent . . . put about, put about . . ."

And then, very faintly, Jack heard a human voice. He could not tell whose it was.

". . . your signal . . . Hello, Jack, we . . . ing . . . about . . . distress . . . can't . . . Jack, do you read . . . Jack . . ."

"I hear you," Jack shouted. "Hold on! I'm coing in! Hesperus, can't you pour more coal into this tub?"

"It would kill you."

"Don't give me that, darn it! Pour it on!"

The lurch of power that followed precluded any further talk. He could barely breathe.

But somebody up there was still alive! In the screen, in fact, he could see that the sail, now little more than a mass of metallic rags, had been reset. The skiff was trying to come around. But by this time it was anything but a responsive vessel. As it turned, it drifted, in the same direction that it had been going before, closer and closer to the center of the cluster.

Beyond it, the peripheries of the Mystery of Mysteries were gradually emerging from the haze of glare into finer focus. Jack, bearing in mind that he had an Angel for an ally, kept his attention strictly on the skiff.

"Starting down on the other side of the curve, now, Jack. The computer says eleven G's for two seconds. Do you know what that means?"

"Yes," Jack said grimly. He detached the oxygen mask from in back of the pilot's chair and put it on, and then strapped over his face the bandage with the two pads for his eyes. Then he inhaled deeply.

"Shoot."

It was as though he had run full tilt into a brick wall. Despite the oxygen, he blacked out.

"Jack. Hello? Hello?"

Jack gasped. The pressure was gone. Hastily he unwrapped the bandage again. Everything around him was floating in a red haze, but he could see details through it; that meant that his retinas hadn't been detached by the deceleration. A sharp pain in his side as he moved told him, however, that he had broken a rib, or at least cracked one.

"How long did that take?" he gasped, doffing the oxygen mask.

"Eight seconds. Deceleration pressure now is slightly over three G's. We will be abreast of your brothers in about thirty-seven minutes."

"And your people? Have you explained to them what we're up to?"

"No, Jack. I do not know myself, except that we are going to intercept your artifact."

That, of course, was perfectly true. There hadn't been time—and it was too late now. Anxiously, Jack peered at the screens.

Despite the deceleration of the *Ariadne,* the skiff was now apparently drawing toward them rather than growing smaller, though the ranging instruments showed that its actual sliding course toward the great cluster of new-born suns had changed very little. One of the outermost of those suns was already near enough to show as a distinct disc in the visiscreen, instead of just a fuzzy point; and small wonder, for it was so young and tenuous that it was nearly half a light year in diameter—the visible disc could be no more than its core, where the torch which would some day become a major star had only just been lit. But though both the skiff and the *Ariadne* were obviously now well within the outer atmosphere of that dim, gigantic infant sun, the remains of the sail of the skiff were still set the same way Jack had seen them last—visibly failing to profit by the additional gusts of energy blowing every which way around and about a newborn star.

Jack refused to think about what that might mean. He concentrated single-mindedly on the task of refining Hesperus' drastic way of flying a spaceship to the delicate job of bringing the *Ariadne* exactly abreast of the skiff.

He was helped a little in this by the fact that the skiff's comet's-tail of Angels seemed to have evaporated at the *Ariadne's* scorching approach—nor, indeed, did the *Ariadne* have such a convoy any more, either. Instead, the whole vast choir of Angels had silently formed a globe of intense red points of light around the Earth vessels, and now enclosed them both in a universe of orbits. It was as if the Angels were waiting for something—to see what he would do, to help him, to hinder him, to destroy them all when the skiff crossed some invisible but sacred boundary line . . . there was no way of guessing.

And right now, Jack suddenly realized, he did not know how he was going to make the skiff fast. It floated now beside the *Ariadne* at a distance of less than a thousand feet, but there seemed to be no way to secure it—and any moment now some random gust of electrons or swirl of gas and dust might strike the tattered sail hard enough to drive the skiff in to a collision or to send it scudding away.

The two spacesuited figures at either end of the keel were silent and motionless. He could no longer hope for any help from that quarter. It was up to him to help them, and fast.

But the *Ariadne* didn't seem to mount any conventional grappling equipment; if she ever had, it had been torn out during Langer's last remodeling job. Where the controls for such equipment would normally be was nothing but a two-pole switch marked LOCKER. The two poles were still labeled ARM and DISARM, but that was obviously only a leftover, meant to stand now for OPEN and SHUT. After all, you couldn't arm a locker . . .

. . . But of course you could, if it were on the outside of the ship to begin with, and specifically designed to cradle another ship, no matter how odd. He threw the switch to the ARM position. Sure enough, the outside locker opened; whether anything else had been accomplished remained to be proven.

"Hesperus, shut down. For this maneuver I don't want anything going but battery power." The Nernst telltale light went out at once, without comment.

At the same time, the skiff began to cant slowly away from him. It looked alarming, but actually it might even be helpful, if it just didn't happen too fast. With infinite gentleness, he eased the *Ariadne* under the heeling skiff and tried, like a man baffled by the last two pieces of a jigsaw puzzle, to fit the skiff's keel into the locker.

It did not quite go. As the I-beam touched the *Ariadne*, the twin lids of the coffinlike locker snapped up on either side of it, and at the same moment all that remained of the sail went whirling away into space in all directions, like so much confetti. The brief storm of foil filled the radar screens with ghosts and made the computer blink and chatter apoplectically.

When the screens had cleared, even the skiff's mile-long "mast" had been reeled in without a trace—and the skiff was secured.

But both Langer and Sandbag were still outside, locked to the I-beam. They did not move, let alone respond to his calls. They had not even anchored their shoes to the hull.

Somebody was going to have to don the other space-suit and go out into that maelstrom after them—whether they were dead or alive. Well, there was only one candidate for the job—and they had taken risks far worse. Now it was up to Jack, under the silent watch of all the Angels in the heavens, and leaving an Angel in sole charge of the *Ariadne* until the task was done.

Or until he failed.

FLIGHT   11

AS HE STOOD in the airlock, in total darkness except for the amber bulb that showed where the lock's little control panel was, he had plenty of time to brood over the hump on the back of his spacesuit and what it implied about the inferno of radiation into which he was about to step. The wait was enforced, even in emergencies: a standard twenty minutes to allow the eyes to become dark-adapted. Even in an emergency, a man who has to grope his way about is of no use; and if there are other people involved, he can be positively dangerous.

At last, however, the amber light turned green, indicating that if he now touched the button to open the outer valve of the airlock, it would respond. The valve opened solemnly, letting in the glow of the cluster.

Now at long last he was seeing the stars raw; and, exactly as he had suspected, the television view of them had lied. First of all, no reproducing system can show a true point-source of light; they all produce a disc, no matter how small. Only the human eye could record and appreciate the piercing glory of a star distant enough to have no diameter at all, yet nevertheless obviously and brilliantly *there*. And the colors! Jack had never dreamed that the eye could be sensitive to color differences so small, because he had never before seen colors without an atmosphere (or some other interference, such as a TV circuit) to modify and blur them. Every single sun in the great panoply before him was distinctly and definitely a different color, for most of which there were no names; the English language, like every other human language, wasn't old enough yet to have accumulated the thousands of adjectives needed to differentiate the colors of space. Even a fashion designer would have been reduced to mute incredulity before such a spectrum; it was as though Jack's eyes had suddenly become highly sensitive spectroscopes, without losing any of their acuity as image formers.

It was hard to believe that he had lived in the wide universe for seventeen years without knowing, until this instant, how gloriously beautiful it was.

And how dangerous.

That price had to be paid. Clumsily, partly because of the hump, but mostly because of his total inexperience at maneuvering in a spacesuit, he edged himself out onto the hull of the *Ariadne*.

Ten feet away from him stood another humpbacked spacesuit, gleaming bluely in the cluster light like a steel statue. No, not even like a statue, for it did not look human; it looked . . . empty. There was not even any white blur behind its faceplate.

Awed and frightened, he forced himself to shuffle toward it. It awaited him stolidly, thick arms hanging at its sides.

It was Langer. His face could not be seen because his head had fallen forward against the faceplate, but even in the darkness inside the helmet Jack could see that it was not Sandbag's crew-cut poll he was staring at. He managed to get the suit unsnapped from the skiff, but then paused indecisively. The radiation counter in his own suit was jammering dementedly, making thinking very difficult. The level was far higher than he had expected, even for this Hades inside the atmosphere of a star. . . .

Induced radioactivity—that was it. The spacesuits and the skiff were hot. There was very little he could do about the suits at the moment, but at least he could get rid of the skiff; it had served its purpose. He found the outside switch for Langer's shoes and left him standing, anchored, while he made his way along the locker to Sandbag.

The cadet's face was ghastly. He was still conscious, but his eyes were rolling from side to side like those of a trapped animal. He seemed wholly unaware of Jack. Could he be trusted not to fumble with the controls of his suit? It had to be chanced. Jack unlocked him from the I-beam, turned on his shoes and shuffled away to hunt down the outside controls for the skiff locker.

It took a back-wrenching heave to get the skiff in motion, even slowly; though it had no weight out here, it still had all its considerable mass. He felt a curious twinge of regret as the bare girder edged away from the *Ariadne* toward the newborn star. The odd vessel had served them gallantly; it could hardly be blamed for the failure of the mission on which it had been sent, yet it was doomed all the same.

Now which of the two men should he take in first? Sandbag was the problem. If he were left outside, he might shut off his shoes before Jack could get to him, or even fire his suit jets; if he were left inside, he might do an immense amount of damage while Jack was pulling in Langer. But something could be done about that—whereas inside the suit, Sandbag was essentially unreachable.

He towed Sandbag after him into the airlock. The cadet made feeble threshing motions, but otherwise did not impede him. The outer valve closed against the glory of the stars.

While he waited for the pumps to bring the air pressure up, Jack broke out the first-aid kit and managed to fumble out a styrette. It was not the instrument he would have preferred, but managing a hypodermic syringe with spacesuit gloves was beyond his skill.

83

The instant the pressure was up, Jack sprang the emergency port on the chest of Sandbag's suit, jabbed the point of the styrette through Sandbag's clothing into his breast muscles, and broke the seal. Only then did he open the inner valve and begin to get the rest of the suit off. By the time he was through, Sandbag was as heavily inert an object as the one after which he had been nicknamed, a massive dose of morphine coursing through his blood stream. Jack left him lying in the well and shoveled his suit back into the airlock; it was too hot to be allowed inside the *Ariadne* for one second longer than could be helped. The moment he got back out onto the hull, he kicked it away after the skiff.

Getting Langer into the ship was a little easier. His suit went in the same direction as Sandbag's.

Now he had to do something for the men.

Langer was, at least, still alive, though both his pulse and his breathing were rapid and shallow. But both of them were sticky and unpleasant—radiation sickness is very much like cholera—and very dehydrated. Jack bundled their clothing into the disposal chute and bathed them, and then strapped them in their bunks, where he set up an intravenous normal-saline continuous injection for both. At this point his medical knowledge ran out and he had to consult the handbook.

The trouble, the handbook said, lay in the bone marrow, about which nothing in the nature of first aid could be done. Immediate hospitalization was the only answer. In the meantime, the book ordered, force fluids—well, he was doing that; give antibiotics to keep down secondary infection—okay; give anti-anemia formulations—were there any on board? Yes, those were the standard vitamin K/vitamin B-12/folic acid/minerals capsules, but how did you give them to unconscious men? A search of the medicine chest failed to turn up any such thing in an injectable form, which was not very surprising, since there was no vehicle tolerable by the body fluids in which all those drugs were mutually soluble. He would have to force the capsules on them if and when they were conscious, otherwise he was helpless. The handbook had nothing else to recommend but chelating agents which were to be used in case the patient had breathed and/or swallowed radioactive particles; but that didn't apply here.

Above all, immediate hospitalization . . . in the heart of the Coal Sack.

"Hesperus!"

"Receiving."

"I promised to take you back to Earth with me, and I will, if Gabriel and the rest of your brothers will let me go. It's imperative that I get back at once. These men we just took aboard are dying. Only treatment on Earth can save them."

There was a pause, but Jack thought he could interpret it. His lucky guess about the attitude of the Angels, a virtually immortal race, toward accidental death, or causing the death of another, had turned out to be correct; life to them was the most precious of all commodities. Well, it was to a short-lived Earthman, too—but that was a fact Earthmen often chose to forget.

"I have spoken with them," Hesperus said. "They will not impede us."

"Good," Jack said, but he felt no corresponding sensation of relief. Though that was not the first fence to be climbed, it was also far from the last. "I'll need your cooperation, too. We're going to have to make the trip on the Standing Wave, because these men couldn't stand the buffeting they'd get from your drive. But I want to go as fast as possible, nonstop; I don't want to take any chances on the hospital facilities at Aaa."

"What is Aaa?"

"Sorry, I was just thinking aloud. The point is, I need every drop of power that can be squeezed out of that fireplace of mine. Can you raise its efficiency much, without blowing us up in the process?"

"I can control it at about ninety-two per cent efficiency, I believe," Hesperus said. "It is much too small to do any better than that with it."

Jack whistled soundlessly. No wonder McCrary and his associates were so anxious to get more Angels working for them. The standard commercial Nernst reactor wasted more than half of the hydrogen fed into it. He had no idea how the *Ariadne* would behave with such a torrent of power available, and furthermore most of the meters couldn't be set high enough to show it; he would inevitably get back to Earth with many of his instruments blown out.

"All right, go to it. I have to work out a course, but in the meantime if we head out toward the rim of the galaxy going north-northeast, we'll at least be headed in the right general direction."

"Okay," Hesperus said.

The Nernst generator promptly began to whine. Jack had never heard a sound out of it before. Lights went out all over the boards; otherwise, nothing happened. Jack got up, growling at himself.

"What is the trouble?" Hesperus said

"You just blew about eighteen fuses. I'm going to have to take most of the fuses out of the circuits and jump them. And pray that the wiring will stand for it."

It took half an hour. Jack fumed at the loss of time, but there was no help for it.

"Okay, Hesperus, go!"

The generator whined again, and power slammed into the Haertel overdrive. The star cluster shrank, dimmed, reddened and vanished in the whirling blackness of the Coal Sack.

By the time Jack had fed his course into the computer, the Sack itself was behind the *Ariadne*— or rather, outside her, as you had to put these matters in Haertel terminology. Inside a Haertel field you were on the Standing Wave, which in a mathematical sense included the whole universe (but in that sense only: the Standing Wave was what was called a topological conform); and as you poured more power into the overdrive, the field selectively rejected the universe, thrust it away from you as intolerable. A Haertel field was very like a rich misanthropist: the richer and more powerful it became, the more jealous it became of its privacy.

Under the riches that Hesperus was supplying it now, it was rejecting the universe at better than two parsecs an hour, or half a trillion miles a minute. It was not real speed, as Langer had been careful to emphasize, since the Standing Wave never went anywhere—it just stood. But it was a good deal better than any possible real speed could have been.

Thereafter, nursing his charges occupied Jack's full time for most of the flight. Langer was not much trouble, for he remained unconscious, barely hovering on the edges of life; Jack would have been more than glad to take more trouble over him, had there been anything he could do. But there was not.

Sandbag, on the other hand, was a terrifying patient. His first indistinct mutter as the morphine began to wear off burgeoned rapidly into a full-throated delirium. It made it almost impossible to feed him, give him his medicine or keep him clean. Still worse, it made it necessary to keep him strapped down, and his repeated lunges against the straps rapidly covered him with enormous purple bruises which would not go away. It was in the nature of his illness to increase the fragility of his blood vessels, so in that sense the bruises were natural—but his illness was also an illness of the bone-marrow tissues that formed his blood cells; he could not afford so much blood loss, even though it was only under his own skin.

And his raving was very hard to live with. Often his subconscious mind, which like that of everyone had never gotten beyond the savagery of apehood, threw out jagged pieces of nightmares so ugly that they were almost impossible to bear. Even at the best, his mumbling and fuming rattled Jack's thinking, and constantly interrupted his few and desperately needed catnaps.

But it had to be borne. Jack had at first been strongly tempted to continue Sandbag under sedation, but had had the good sense to check the handbook first. The handbook said *No* in the firmest possible way; many an incautious doctor or first-aid amateur had turned patients into morphine addicts that way; try the amylobarbitone, vial XI-237. Jack tried it, but it did not improve the situation much—it did subdue Sandbag somewhat, but it also seemed to confuse him even more. The only other available drug was a short-term anesthetic called hydroxydione, but the handbook's instructions on how to give this to the patient were so hedged around with warnings about possible irritation of the veins that Jack was afraid to try it. Better the devil you know than the devil you don't.

Still, it was tempting, for the opening passage about the drug read: *Hydroxydione is the natural body hormone controlling normal sleep. It may be given with large margins of safety if the following precautions against thrombosis are observed. . . .* No. Leave that kind of thing to licensed physicians . . . if they could be gotten to in time.

The best medicine Jack and Hesperus could give their two patients now was speed.

The thought reminded him that in all this sweating round of nursing chores, he had lost track of where they were. Doubtless they were on course, and their translation time matched to the power Hesperus was pouring out of the Nernst generator, otherwise the computer would have called him. But neither Hesperus nor the computer had any way of matching course

87

time against the ebbing of a human life. He strapped Sandbag back down securely and hurried forward to the screens.

The plot position indicator showed that more than half the trip was done; there was also a little strip of tape which was a challenge from the station on Aaa, radically incomplete. Evidently Hesperus, on his own initiative, had flicked the *Ariadne* off the Standing Wave for a second or so as she was passing that system. Jack had never even felt it. Hesperus was learning to smooth the Haertel overdrive into his own.

"Hesperus?"

"Receiving."

"Why did you go off overdrive by Aaa?"

"I wanted to see what it was, because you had mentioned it when we started. If it was important you might need a message from it."

Jack grinned in spite of himself, scanning the tape. "You didn't give them a chance. This is just a little piece of a standard challenge. You must have scared them blue."

There was a small clicking sound. "How did you deduce that?"

"What? You've lost me."

"That what you call blue is a color of alarm," Hesperus explained patiently.

"Oh. Well, I didn't." He thought about it a minute. "Protoplasmic people tend to lose their pink color when they're alarmed, and I suppose that some kind of retinal afterimage makes them look bluish or greenish to the observer. I really don't know much about that kind of thing. Listen, Hesperus, can you give me a look outside—particularly astern? I can see where we are on the PPI scope, but I want to look at the stars."

"You can look at any time, Jack. We are on the Standing Wave now, not on my drive."

Feeling silly, Jack snapped on the viewscreens, which provided a converted and adjusted image of normal space through the Haertel field. Of course on Hesperus' drive they would have shown nothing at all, because traveling faster than light in normal space makes sight impossible; but what with his worries about his patients, and the fragmentary message from Aaa, he had become thoroughly disoriented.

Seconds later, he had the *Ariadne* placed in space; and he no longer felt even the least bit foolish. He was, instead, terrified.

To the stern, the Coal Sack had dwindled into little more than the hole in the Milky Way which had shown itself to Earthly sailors even before the age of telescopes—but it and the Milky Way both were almost masked by point-sources of sullen red light.

Behind the *Ariadne,* following her easily on the Standing Wave toward Earth, were clouds and clouds of Angels.

SIEGE 12

AFTER THE FIRST shock, Jack was surprised to discover that he was not really entirely surprised. Surely this mass migration of the Angels from their dark nest was alarming, but somewhere in the bottom of his mind he had expected it.

He had made a treaty with them, and they were following him home to fulfill their obligations. They did not know how many years it might take to get that treaty ratified—years were less than minutes to them—nor that mankind could not possibly be ready to put them to work the instant the agreement was made. They were following Earth's ambassador home, sure that everything had already been settled.

And there was precisely nothing he could do about it. No attempt to explain the real situation to them, through Hesperus, could head them off now. It would just ruin the agreement instead.

Or had there really been any agreement? How could you be sure, when one of the parties was not made of flesh and was almost as old as time itself? This pursuit of Angels might mean something much worse for Earth than Jack's mind, trained to think first of all in terms of space law and diplomacy, could manage on short notice to imagine.

Behind him, in the well, there was a low, fluttering moan. There were no words to go with it, but the voice was Langer's. He had made that sound before; but there was always the chance that, *this* time, he might struggle up to consciousness and explain to Jack what he ought to be doing. Jack abandoned the boards to tend to him.

But Langer only moaned once more and resumed his shallow breathing, his eyes shuttered in his shadowed face.

Jack was still in charge.

The *Ariadne,* obediently following its computer, snapped off the Standing Wave just inside the orbit of Uranus, and instantly was flying at less than a third of the speed of light and losing speed fast. At the same time, the computer began to send out her recognition signal—but this time, nothing could have been more unnecessary, for all the Angels came off the Standing Wave at the same instant.

Suddenly, the solar system was the target of the greatest comet in the history of man, a fiery arrow already past the three outermost rings, and homing fast toward the bull's-eye. It sprang into existence in the sky of the inhabited planets without the slightest warning, and the homing signals of the *Ariadne* were swamped out in an unprecedented storm of radio static.

Between nursing bouts, Jack fought to get some kind of signal down to Secretary Hart, through the roar of the Angels and the howls of alarm that were passing back and forth—or trying to—between the inner planets. It didn't work. He had the *Ariadne's* Nernst generator and all the unprecedented efficiency that Hesperus could bring it to; but there were the great fusion reactors of Earth, Mars, Venus, the four Jovian satellites, Titan, and the outpost satellites all the way out to Proserpine II competing with him, and untold thousands of the Angels from the Coal Sack competing with Hesperus. He could neither hear nor be heard; in the uproar, the *Ariadne* herself passed above the asteroid belt undetected, though Jack was shouting himself hoarse. Behind him, Sandbag came out from under sedation again and began to shout, too.

Then, suddenly, somebody in the solar system took charge. All the planets stopped transmitting, starting with Earth, and going silent one after the other, at the speed of light, until the wave of silence reached and passed Proserpine, the tenth planet. Jack had no idea what was happening, but the wave of silence had in it the sound of authority. He cut out the *Ariadne's* transmitter and waited, listening to the static of the Angels, hardly daring to breathe. In the background, Sandbag groaned and tossed and muttered.

Earth calling. (Awk! Rrr.) . . . *ing. Earth calling.*

Jack's hand leaped for the transmitter switch and halted. He hadn't been able to get through to them, but they had figured out something; better just to listen, and hope.

. . . *and heterodyne. We will reinforce.* (Cchh. Rrrr.) . . . *in*

90

five seconds. Tick will begin in five seconds. (Rrrrch.) *Send in bursts on each tick and we will reinforce. Repeat:* (Oooowowooo . . . Rchcrhch.) *. . . calling. Earth calling . . .*

Magically, the static of the Angels began to diminish, until finally there was nothing to be heard from the speakers on the boards but the sound of the stars, that noise of chaos which the poet John Milton called "the dismal universal hiss." Milton had never heard it, nor did anybody until two centuries after him, but nobody has ever described it better.

Then, from Earth to Proserpine, there began the long pulses of carrier waves, and the Angels picked them up. Inside the *Ariadne*, Hesperus caught them and fed them into the ship's transmitter.

"Transmit, Jack. Some entity is calling you."

Convulsively, Jack tried once more to send the recognition signal.

Pulse. Pulse. Pulse.

"Howie! Howie, is that you? Hello *Ariadne!*"

Pulse.

"Hello, Secretary Hart, Jack Loftus here."

Pulse. Pulse.

"Hello, Jack, thank God. Put Dr. Langer on. We're . . ." Pulse. ". . . hysterics down here. Get him on quick."

Pulse. Pulse.

"Mr. Hart, I can't. He's dying. Please get us down quick. I need a course, I can't do it myself."

Pulse. Pulse.

"Jack, that's too slow, too. Get Jerry Stevens to do it for you. It's worth the chance. We can't risk your piloting now."

Pulse.

"Secretary Hart, please—Sandbag's dying, too. Send me a course, or it'll all have been for nothing!"

Pulse. Pulse.

"Jack . . . What about these Angels? Is it safe? Do we dare bring the *Ariadne* down?"

Pulse. Pulse. Pulse. Pulse. Pulse. Pulse. Pulse.

"Secretary Hart," Jack said with a heavy heart, "you don't dare not to."

Pulse. Pulse.

"All right. Stand by, Jack. I knew you'd make it. You'll have a landing orbit in about a minute and a half. Stand by." (Rchch. Rrrr.) "Jack"

"Yes, sir."

"Hold on," Secretary Hart's voice said proudly. "I will get you down, no matter what. Do you hear? No matter what."

Overwhelmed, Jack signed off. A few minutes later, the computer began to tick and chatter with the incoming elements of the landing orbit it was receiving from Alvarez Field. The *Ariadne* resettled herself in space and began to descend, none too gently, toward the Earth.

"Jack?"

"Receiving," Jack said, exhausted.

"I have been listening," Hesperus said. "They have love for you in your nest."

Jack looked over his shoulder at the great comet of Angels.

"I guess they do," he said, sadly. "But I kind of doubt that it'll last."

There was no doubt in Jack's mind that the approach of this vast ghostly horde was creating consternation on the Earth—though that was pure deduction on his part, since with the special communication pulses now halted, he could again get nothing on the radio but static. However, he was human; that was all he needed. He knew in particular that the large majority of the populace of the world had never heard of the Angels—not because their existence had been kept secret, or because the controversy over them had not been more or less fully aired; but because vast numbers of people have no access to the news of the day, and of those who do only a small proportion ever pay attention to any story that does not generate large headlines. Up to now, the Angels had not been that big a story.

Now they were more than a story. They were a visible reality, and a frightening one, and—for most people—a totally new and inexplicable one. Probably the news was being blared out now at top speed and volume, but it would be a while before the stories caught up with the thing itself.

Freed of the task of piloting, Jack had nothing to do but watch while the computer tooled the *Ariadne* down through the atmosphere toward Alvarez. As the ship descended, the hash on the radio began to dwindle, until faint voices from Earth stations were coming through it. This was the first hint that Jack had that the Angels were not going to follow him all the way down to the ground; but after only a few minutes more, he could confirm it by eye. Instead, they were forming themselves into a vast lurid shell around the Earth, about halfway between the outermost limits of the atmosphere and the orbit of the Moon.

It was very much like the twinkling sphere that they had formed around the *Ariadne* while he was rescuing his friends from the derelict of the photon-skiff. And it was just as difficult to interpret. Jack could only hope that this time, too, they would follow a policy of nonintervention—but it was impossible to erect a trend from one example.

At least radio communication inside the atmosphere would be possible, as long as the Angels maintained their shell outside the Kennelly-Heaviside layer. On the other hand, radio between the planets was utterly cut off. Did the Angels intend that? Did they even know it? Well, he could always ask Hesperus.

The *Ariadne* touched ground, and was almost instantly surrounded by soldiers. A medical detachment pushed through the cordon. With a sigh of relief and exhaustion, Jack opened the airlock for them.

They examined Langer and Sandbag very thoroughly, but very swiftly too, before deciding how to move them, or whether or not they could be moved at all, while a Medical Corps major crisply extracted from Jack everything that he knew.

"Um. Well, Mr. Loftus, we have two things on our side. First, that you got them home as fast as you did. Second, that you obeyed the fundamental law of medicine: *Primum non nocere.*"

"I did? I never heard of it. What does it mean?"

"It means," the major said, "'First, do no harm.' Someone else in your position might have been tempted to experiment. You had the good sense to know that you didn't know. All right, boys, get hammocks for the patients, and do it gently. I want them to get to the hospital without one single new bruise. But snappily."

As they worked, swiftly but with infinite gentleness, Sandbag began to mutter again.

"Major, can we give this one a little Viadril jolt?"

"No. I said no bruises—not even a needle puncture."

"Right."

Jack felt as though he had finally been allowed to shed a lead cloak he had been wearing for weeks. He wiped his forehead and slumped in the control chair.

"You look none too well yourself, Mr. Loftus. Here; get yourself a cup of water and bolt this down."

"I don't need anything." Jack objected. "I'm just relieved, that's all. Now if I can just get a little sleep—"

"But you can't," the major said quietly. "So you'd better let me judge what you need. You are ordered to board a jet for Washington directly from here; Secretary Hart wants to see you, soonest. Take the pill and don't argue, because it won't get you anywhere. I've been a military surgeon for twenty years—I'm used to dealing with heroes."

He looked it. Jack swallowed the pill resignedly, and left the *Ariadne*. Probably he would never see her again. Now it was up to him to explain to Secretary Hart what had happened in the Coal Sack, as best he could. Privately, he doubted that the pill would be of much help.

OTHER EYES ARE WATCHING   13

SECRETARY HART was alone when Tim Bearing admitted Jack to the office. Once more the sunlight was bright, and all the past seemed dreamlike—all the more so for the drug coursing through his blood stream, which kept him awake, but made him feel oddly untethered from reality.

He was only a month older now than he had been when it had all begun. It did not seem possible.

"Sit down, Jack," the Secretary said heavily. "Before we begin, let me say that I'm proud of you. You're the best justification of the cadet system yet to find its way onto the books."

"Thank you, sir. But it's a bad situation. You may not feel very happy about it—or about me—when you hear the whole story."

Hart snorted. "I'm highly unhappy about it already; but that doesn't alter anything I said. Well, well, go ahead; let's have it."

Slowly, and with a good deal of groping for words where there did not really seem to be any human terms to describe what had happened, Jack told his history.

"About the treaty, if that was what it was," he added, "I had the tape going so you can hear what I said. But I haven't had a chance to play it back, so I don't know whether or not Gabriel recorded. I could hear him and I presume the recorder could, but I don't know."

"That doesn't worry me," the Secretary said. "Your friend Hesperus can give it back to us verbatim if we need it—provided of course that we can persuade the Secretary-General to trust him or any other Angel."

"What makes you think he could, sir? Hesperus, I mean?"

"Why, that's obvious. No creature can live four million years, let alone from the beginning of time, without a perfect memory. Either that, or he'd have to do without a mind at all, like a vegetable—a giant redwood, for instance. Your own memory is perfect, Jack, and you'll only live a hundred years or so."

"My memory," Jack said ruefully, "is as full of holes as a sieve. I thought I was going to be able to play back the talk about the treaty word for word, but it's already gone all fuzzy."

"We can get it out of you word for word if we have to. It's only your conscious mind that forgets. Your unconscious preserves a perfect and unvariable record of every single fact you have ever observed. Everybody's does. But it would be easier and safer to get the details from Hesperus if we have to; playing back the subconscious memory involves stereotaxic surgery on the brain, which we don't like to do unless it's absolutely unavoidable. But it can be done."

Jack blinked. "Do you mean that you could go back to some tiny little thing that I saw when I was three years old—like a brick wall, say—and make me count the bricks and tell you which of them was cracked, and so on? Even if I wasn't paying any conscious attention to the wall when I saw it?"

"Yes, Jack. The unconscious misses nothing, and it never forgets. However, let's not worry any more about that until we see how complete your tapes are. Right now, what I want is your assessment of what's important about what happened to you—something the unconscious can't do, for it's totally devoid of judgment. I gather you've given me all that."

"Yes, sir," Jack said. "I think so. But I'm awfully tired and mixed up. I may think of something else later."

"Don't worry. This is a good start." Hart frowned and put his forefingers against his eyebrows. He did not look nearly as confident as his words sounded. "Well, let's see what this adds up to. I do wish we had Howard here, but we don't, so that's that."

"Sir . . . is Dr. Langer going to live?"

"I wish I knew. But let's stick to the point. I'm inclined to feel that you handled an almost intolerable situation as well as anyone could have done. Maybe Howard would have handled it better, I don't know; the fact is that he badly misjudged it at the beginning and that's why he's on the critical list now, and Jerry Stevens with him. A lesson for hero-worshipers: *nobody* is right every time."

He paused. He looked so harrowed and sad that Jack felt ashamed to have thought that he himself had ever had a trouble in the world.

"All right. Now I must be frank to tell you that however it looks to me, it looks very bad to the public, whose servant I am. In the light of what has happened—especially this investment of the Earth by the Angels, and the cutting off of interplanetary communications, and much, much more—I am going to be hard put to it to defend you. And not only you, but the whole cadet system itself. The man in the street is impatient of diplomacy, just as he's impatient of other forms of politics; he thinks that our customs and procedures are mostly rituals that could be cut across by shaking a fist, talking tough, using common sense, and so on. He has the same distrust of lawyers, except when he needs one. Not his fault, maybe; politicians have the habit of appealing to this prejudice of his when they want re-election, instead of honestly trying to explain that some decisions are hard come by and can't be covered in a newspaper editorial in one-syllable words. As for the cadet system, it looks awfully like an in-group to the man whose children are excluded. He would rather think the exams and so on are fakery than accept that his Johnny can't pass them and that the requirements are designed to meet real situations. And when the office involved is appointive, like mine, rather than one the common man was allowed to influence by his ballot—then there's real fury invoked, and no place for it to light on."

"I remember," Jack said. "That's why we study the American Secretaries of State. Everybody hated them no matter what their party was—Seward, Acheson, Dulles, all of them. Yet they were mostly pretty good—not perfect, but good."

"Yes. The poor ones were men like Herter, who *didn't* arouse any passions among the electorate, because essentially they never did anything to arouse disagreement. However, we're wandering; we had better get back to what *we* are up against. I am already under heavy pressure on this Coal Sack affair. The press, which never paid any attention to the Angels when the problem was more or less technical, suddenly wants to know how I allowed all these Angels to put the Earth in siege. It's a good question and I have no answer for it. Trans-Stellar is being particularly tough with me about it, as you might expect. As for the know-nothing press—which will be with us until the end of time, I suspect—they didn't even know that the Angels existed until now, and now it's too late to try to explain it to them all over again.

"Finally, there is McCrary. His corporation will inevitably claim that I have grossly mishandled the matter, from the beginning. Trans-Stellar is already calling upon the UN to oust me from my office. This is a standard ploy, but it's standard because sometimes it works. With public terror of the unknown behind it, it has an excellent chance of working. And with no competent witness but a cadet—that's you, Jack—I am relatively defenseless. I'll fight, sure; but I'm short on weapons."

Jack swallowed. "If Dr. Langer—"

"*If* Dr. Langer. Yes. But we have no assurance that he'll recover in time to help us—or that he'll recover at all. In the meantime, the next step is going to be a board of inquiry, and Jack, you are going to be its target . . . its immediate target. The ultimate target will be the cadet system itself, but so far as the Coal Sack is concerned you are the only witness to what happened."

"Sir, there's Hesperus."

"Jack, I'm sorry, but Hesperus has no status as a witness in a UN court; if you weren't so exhausted you'd know that yourself. We're on our own. I will appear for you, of course. So will a great many other people who have a stake in the cadet system, and the present educational system as a whole. You'll have all the expert help we can possibly give you. But we have all been on Earth all the time. We have not witnessed the crucial parts of the story; and we all have lost prestige and credibility by the outcome—the visible outcome, this frightening shell of Angels around the Earth. Jack, you've done nobly; but the hardest part is yet to come, and you are going to have to do that, too."

Jack thought about it, but he was too weary to take it all in. In a way it was a sad and rather deadening anticlimax, after the high drama of his tense, emotion-charged dialogue with Gabriel in the birthplace of stars; it seemed like quibbling. Yet his training had taught him that the fates of peoples and nations often rested upon finer and finer distinctions, upon the making of new amendments to old laws, upon commas and changes of tense and slight changes of emphasis, as a kite gains stability with each new knot that is tied in its tail. It would be more satisfying to draw an atom bomb and go *bang!* each time a thing of this kind came up, but that didn't solve problems, it only obliterated them: the Patrick Henry syndrome, emotionally stated as *Give me liberty or give me death*, but at bottom meaning only *Agree with me or I'll kill us both.*

"I'll tell the story as many times as they want me to," he said slowly. "I don't know what else I can do. It probably won't help much."

"No, probably not. It might make a difference if Howard could testify, but I won't risk his life, Jack; strange though it may seem to you, this is not the last crisis the Earth may go through, and if I have to save Howard's life by keeping him off the stand on this inquiry, I will do so, no matter how crucial his testimony might be. Do you understand that?"

"I guess I do. Dr. Langer isn't expendable."

"Yes. He was wrong this time. But I will need him next time all the same. As for Jerry, his chances look much better; but I can't see that anything he might tell the board of inquiry will be of any real help without Howard to back him up. Can you?"

"Ummm. No. Not really. Unless he saw something in the Coal Sack that I didn't see. And even then, unless Dr. Langer saw it too—This is a mess, isn't it?"

Unexpectedly, Secretary Hart grinned. "That's what makes it fun, Jack."

"Fun?"

"Sure. Nothing's more fun than reducing noise to some kind of order. If all problems came to you in a package, you'd die of boredom, and so would the race. Cheer up, and let's cope. Coping is the greatest game of all. People who don't know that aren't really people at all; they're cabbages."

After a moment, Jack began to laugh. It wasn't precisely the way he had seen the drama; but suddenly it struck him as the only way to look at it. It made him feel older, and made him enjoy it. Of course the situation was serious; otherwise, why care about it at all?

Secretary Hart read his expression, and nodded.

"So, let's proceed. We now have to come up on the board of inquiry, as best we can. In the meantime, the diplomatic situation, which is what is *really* important—whatever the press thinks—may be simply standing in abeyance, or it may be getting steadily worse. Thus far we have no way of knowing which. All we do know is that the Angels are still out there, and they are still waiting silently to see what we'll do.

98

"But obviously they won't wait forever. It's up to us. Are you with it?"

"Yes, sir. To the end of the line."

"Good," Secretary Hart said, with a gentle smile. "We haven't much time; better go to your quarters and get your sleep. The board of inquiry meets tomorrow."

QUESTIONS 14

SOMEBODY HAD ABSENT-MINDEDLY booked the board of inquiry meeting for a Senate committee room in Washington, and it had to be pointed out to him that this was not precisely a matter of American interest alone. Jack never found out who did the booking, but there was no doubt about who did the pointing, because he did it publicly: it was the President of the United States. The meeting was hastily transferred to the chambers of the Security Council, in New York.

Only then did Jack begin to realize exactly what they were up against. Until now, he had not stopped to ask himself who in the world had the right to put an American cabinet officer—a man technically in line for the presidency, given a rather unlikely series of accidents—on the griddle. The answer was now before him, seated in a row at the gently curved bench:

The President himself; the Secretary-General; the Security Council, minus its American representative. The President was sitting for him.

In the old days it would have turned out very differently. Then it would have been the Senate of the United States who grilled the cabinet officer, who would then have resigned, whether right or wrong, so as not to be an embarrassment to the administration of which he was a part. Today the United States was more conservative of good cabinet officers, who are hard to come by; hence Secretary Hart was given the best representation on the Council that the country could offer. Whether or not that was going to be good enough was another question.

And it meant, Jack realized with a chill, that the President was also going to be questioning *him*.

He was sure his parents were watching. The whole world was. Television cameras peered at the rostrum from every possible angle, including almost directly overhead, and the press section was bulging. In it he saw Sylvia, murmuring to a male colleague about twice Jack's age, who was trying unsuccessfully to look bored. When she saw Jack looking at her she smiled—evidently she was not holding any grudge over the encounter on Aaa—but he did not smile back. It had been her father who had started this whole avalanche rolling, and what part she had played in it was anything but clear.

Sylvia transferred her smile to Sandbag, with an ease meant to suggest that it had been him she had been smiling at all along. He waved, but it was plain to see that his heart wasn't in it. He was not long out of the hospital in any event, and was still somewhat weak; but he had assured Secretary Hart that he was up to the ordeal, and the doctors somewhat doubtfully agreed.

They were sitting with the Secretary and his aides, a round dozen of them. Langer was not with them. He was still on the critical list, incommunicado.

"How did your boss manage to get so much heavier a dose than you did?" Jack asked.

"Jack, I don't know. He was never out of my sight; anything that hit him should have hit me. Maybe it's just that he's older than I am and his resistance is lower?"

"Close," Secretary Hart said tersely. "The fact is that he's been in space for many more years than you have, and it's the total dose that counts. Quiet down, now; they're beginning."

The Secretary-General leaned forward to the microphone.

"We will now call the Honorable Daniel Hart, Secretary for Space."

Hart stood up. There was no witness stand, for this was not officially a trial. It had all the atmosphere of one, however.

"Secretary Hart, the Council has read the position paper with which your office supplied us, giving your account of the mission to the Greater Coal Sack nebula. We understand that the senior officer of that mission cannot appear."

"I regret very much that he cannot, Mr. Nilssen," Hart said. "He is gravely ill."

"Can't he at least submit a statement?" the representative for Peru asked.

"His physicians will not allow us to talk to him at all. We understand that he is under heavy sedation."

"In any event, we understand that actual negotiations with these aliens now investing the planet were conducted by a cadet," the representative for the Soviet Union said.

"One such negotiation was, Mr. Richter. That cadet is with us today. If Dr. Langer also negotiated with the Angels we have no way of knowing it at present, except indirectly. The evidence is that he did not."

"And it's your position, Dan, that we ought to stand back of the agreement concluded by this young man?" the President asked.

"Yes, sir. Regardless of his age, he conducted the affair—one of monumental delicacy, as I'm sure the Council will appreciate—as creditably as anyone could have; and insofar as we can be sure, the Angels regard him as a proper representative and the agreement as binding."

Jack saw Sylvia whispering to another reporter. He frowned and shook his head. She moved on to still another man. It was impossible to know what she was up to, of course, but it looked as if she were pulling wires again.

"Mr. Secretary, I have to say that my country regards this as an incredible position," said the representative for France. "It should be clear to all humanity at this point that if these energy creatures are hostile, the Earth is utterly at their mercy. To depend for their good will on a rather murky agreement drawn up by a boy is absurd. It is more than absurd; it is madness."

"If you will permit me, sir," Secretary Hart said, "the agreement is without precedent, but there is nothing in the least murky about it. In fact, Mr. Loftus' negotiations with them constitute a whole new principle of diplomacy, which may well open a new era in interstellar relations as a whole. We have been invited to step into a new age—an age of total trust. We can do no less than show that humanity is now mature enough to live in that age and with that principle. The stakes, let me assure you, are incalculable."

"That is more than visible," the representative for France said dryly. He had of course taken Hart to be referring to the waiting cloud of Angels. Jack wondered why the Secretary was still keeping the secret of the galactic federation, but after a moment he thought he knew. Humanity still had many thousands of years to go before it would know whether or not it had passed *that* test; the fact that a virtual eternity had been cut to half an eternity—or might be—would not impress a roomful of national leaders with an immediate doom hanging over them, and over their watching and listening peoples.

"Then I call your attention, sir, to the fact that this is our last chance to show the Angels that we treated with them in good faith."

"I would be more impressed with this position," the representative for the Soviet Union said, "if the officer in charge of the mission had been responsible for the agreement."

"He would support it, I am sure. He will support it, when he is able. But by then it may be too late."

"Can his subaltern tell us nothing at all?" the Secretary-General said. "The Council ought to question him, at least."

"Certainly. Mr. Nilssen, Cadet Gerald Stevens."

Sandbag stood up. He had never looked less flippant in his life.

"Mr. Stevens," the President said, "did Mr. Langer ever talk to the aliens at all while you were together in the cloud?"

"No, sir. We were on our way to what we took to be their center of government when Cadet Loftus intercepted us."

"What for?" said the representative from France.

"Because we had made a mistake, sir. What we were heading for was actually a sort of religious center. It would have caused all kinds of trouble if we'd actually gotten there."

"This is merely an assumption," said the representative for Peru. "None of you actually knows."

"Well, sir, we can't prove it," Sandbag admitted. "But we were on the scene, sir, and we were pretty convinced of it."

There was a flurry of scribbling in the press section. Sylvia was no longer visible, which worried Jack for no reason he could name. If she was supposed to be covering the hearing for her employers, she had picked a bad time to duck out.

"Isn't it true, Mr. Stevens," the representative for France was saying, "that your record for good judgment is in any event not entirely clear?"

Sandbag flushed, but before he could answer, Secretary Hart was on his feet. "Mr. Nilssen, forgive me for interrupting, but I cannot permit Cadet Stevens to answer that. The incident to which M. Savarin refers was a normal training incident and is so entered in my department's records; rehashing it here would serve no purpose. Let me point out that the cadet was on the mission with the full confidence of his senior officer, Dr. Langer, and as far as we know he has it still. He has mine as well."

The question was not pressed, but the press scribbled still faster. If what the board, the press and the public were looking for was a scapegoat, Jack thought grimly, they had found one. After a few more questions, furthermore, it became clear that

Sandbag had essentially nothing to add to what the Council already knew, and he was allowed to sit down.

"We will call Cadet John Loftus," the Secretary-General said. His heart pounding, Jack stood up.

"Mr. Loftus," said the representative for Peru, "what assurance do you have that these energy creatures will abide by any agreement you have concluded with them?"

"I have their word, sir."

"No documents?"

"A tape recording of the conversations, sir. I believe Secretary Hart has supplied the Council with a dub of it."

"But this is still just talk," the representative from France objected. "If we ask, 'What good is their word?' we are left just where we were before."

"Sir," Jack said, "in all the conversations that I had with the Angels, none of them ever told me anything less than the exact truth, at all times."

"This in itself might make them rather difficult to live with," the representative for the Soviet Union said. "But it seems rather unlikely."

"It is my experience, sir," Jack said doggedly. "If they say they will keep an agreement, that is what they mean. I am sure they would not mind signing a document if that is what's required, but—sir, I mean no impertinence—but how would they hold a pen?"

There was some nervous laughter in the audience at this, in which the representative from the Soviet Union joined; but it was rather grim laughter on his part, Jack thought.

The representative from Peru was passed a note; he read it and passed it to the Secretary-General. During the pause, Jack heard whispering behind him, and turned to see Sylvia in animated conference with Secretary Hart's legal staff. The Secretary himself looked both stunned and wrathful, but after a moment he got to his feet.

"Mr. Nilssen, I seem to be cast in the role of perpetual interrupter, but a matter of great importance has just arisen. Though it is most irregular, we have with us a sort of ancillary witness, a newspaperwoman, who has a statement to read on our behalf."

Nilssen looked surprised, but he said, "Proceed."

Jack sat down and Sylvia stood before the microphone.

"Sir, I'm Sylvia McCrary of Trans-Stellar Press," she said in a clear voice. "I have, entirely unethically, used my credentials and

103

some external influence I have available to see Dr. Howard Langer." There was a roar of amazement. "His doctors were unaware of it as far as I know, until now. I was fortunate enough to find him conscious for a brief while, and I have a statement from him."

The roar of amazement got louder, despite the banging of Nilssen's gavel. The Council put all its heads together.

"You," Jack shot at Sylvia, "are in a jam."

"I know it," she said. "I'll be lucky not to wind up in jail. I only hope it was worth it."

"Well, if anybody tells me you haven't got guts, I'll bop him one!"

Nilssen banged the gavel again. "The Council has ruled that this statement, though unethically obtained and irregularly introduced, is admissible under the circumstances. You may read it."

That, Jack realized, had been inevitable. Langer was a public hero, the world over.

"It says: 'I am told that there exists an agreement between the Angels and the Earth, drawn by Cadet John Loftus. I do not know the text of the agreement, but I have full confidence in Cadet Loftus and regard the agreement as binding. Signed, Howard K. Langer.'"

"Is this document sworn?" the representative from France demanded.

"No, sir, there wasn't time. He wasn't conscious long enough. He was barely able to sign it."

"Miss McCrary, are you related to Paul X. McCrary?" said the representative for Peru.

"He is my father," Sylvia admitted.

"Then do you not realize that your intervention in this affair is hopelessly compromised?" the Peruvian demanded.

"Not in my own eyes," Sylvia said firmly. "I acted on my own initiative. My father has nothing to do with it and knew nothing about it."

"I am afraid," the President said, not unkindly, "that you have rather put your foot in it, Miss McCrary. In any event, this doesn't resolve the central question of whether or not the Angels will keep their word. As Dr. Langer never talked to them, he couldn't corroborate Cadet Loftus' testimony in any event."

"But there is someone here who can," Sylvia said. She turned and cried, "Hesperus!"

A ball of shining flame floated into the chamber. There was panic.

"It's only fair," Sylvia shouted above the clamor, "that you listen to both sides!"

ANSWERS 15

THE UPROAR WENT on for nearly ten minutes. Many people broke for the door; but after a while, as it became evident that the Angel was simply floating in mid-air without making any aggressive moves at all, they began to drift back.

From the black expression on Secretary Hart's face, Jack could see that Sylvia had not told him of this part of her program. Nor was it at all clear that the Council was going to have any part of it. One of the people who had fled was the representative from France, and it didn't seem that he was coming back, either.

Jack grabbed at Sylvia's arm. "How did you do it? Hesperus can't hear!"

She opened her hand. In it was a tiny transistorized transceiver. "I snitched it from Dad. He uses it to talk to Lucifer. Of course I couldn't get anywhere near the *Ariadne*, but I stood on the edge of the spaceport and took the chance that Hesperus could receive me from there, and he did."

The noise got louder, and there was a new commotion at the door. Jack stood up on a chair to peer over the heads of the churning mob; all semblance of order had now vanished.

It was Langer.

He was being borne down the aisle toward the rostrum on a stretcher, carried by two husky wardboys in white ducks. His face was white and sunken and he looked ten years older, but his eyes burned.

Hart pushed forward to help clear the way, but not without shooting a murderous glance at Sylvia. After a while, they had lowered Langer gently into a chair next to the Secretary's.

"Howard, why did you do it? You're killing yourself!"

"Far from it. Those conservative medicos of yours were playing it too safe. And as soon as I realized what Sylvia was planning to do, I threw some weight around. But get me the floor, will you? I'm under a stimulant now but I don't know how long it'll last."

Hart nodded and signaled to Nilssen. After a while, the room began to quiet; the very presence of Langer seemed to be radiating through it.

"Dr. Langer," the Secretary-General said, "we are honored."

"Thank you, Mr. Nilssen. I should not be here, as you are aware, and I would not be here were we not all confronted with a truly momentous crisis. I want to point out to you that since Miss McCrary's good offices are not free of irregularities, you have with you only one person, and he is the only person in the world, who can communicate with the Angels about the situation as it now stands. That man is Cadet Loftus. You are standing on the brink of disaster—or of a new era in interstellar relations. You owe it to humanity not to deprive it of a spokesman at this crucial moment."

As he spoke another Angel drifted into the room; then another. The Council eyed them with expressions ranging from misgiving to outright fright.

"I think you had better advise us, Dr. Langer," Nilssen said. "Obviously something has got to be done. But what?"

"I suggest that you stand down," Langer said in an iron voice. "You cannot speak for mankind now. You will have to yield in favor of Jack Loftus, and I suggest that you do it in a hurry. Jack, take that radio of Sylvia's and get busy; you know the questions the Council wants answered; ask them."

Now there were six Angels floating in the chamber.

"Very well," Nilssen said shakily.

Jack could not tell one Angel from the other. He turned Sylvia's transceiver up to full volume and said, "Hesperus?"

"Receiving." The Council jumped, in a body. Evidently they had not really believed, after all, that these creatures were sentient and intelligent. "We are ready, Jack."

"Ready for what? What's the purpose of this gathering?"

"To sign the treaty. I have been reporting what I sense here, and we conclude that the grand agreement is now prepared. Is that not so?"

"Almost," said Jack, restraining himself forcibly from crossing his fingers in public. "These men here are leaders of humanity. They would like me to ask you some questions."

"We understand. Proceed."

"Uh—whom do we have here on your side, besides yourself?"

"The two you call Gabriel and Lucifer, plus three more of the First-Born."

"Sir," Jack said, turning to the Secretary-General, "the First-Born are those Angels who were created during the first twenty minutes of the creation of the entire universe. Do you accept these as responsible delegates for the race of Angels as a whole? I can seek another spokesman if you wish it; Hesperus himself is a cadet Angel, only four million years old."

"Only!" Nilssen said. He was obviously staggered. "Please, Mr. Loftus. go on."

"Hesperus, the Council welcomes the First-Born as one group of leaders to another, and is ready to treat with you if you are ready."

"Do you speak for them, Jack?"

Jack floundered for a moment; it was an impossible position to be put in—a cadet vouching for the Security Council, and the President of the United States!

But the President himself rescued him. "Jack, chin up. You're in the driver's seat. They trust you. Tell him we're okay."

Jack squared his shoulders. "Yes, Hesperus, I speak for them."

"Ask him," the representative for Peru put in, "why they have raised this army against us."

"I don't think—" Jack began, and then reconsidered. It was not what he thought that counted now. He put the question to Hesperus, verbatim.

There was the briefest of puzzled silences.

"There is no army," Hesperus said. "We have brought with us our young, as Gabriel said we would do. Those who wish to work for you will stay; the others will return to the nursery."

"The nursery is where Mr. McCrary's disabled ship is," Jack added. "It was too hot to salvage, and they were playing with it, anyhow."

"Oh," said the representative for Peru, somewhat hollowly.

"There seem to be no more questions," Jack told Hesperus.

"Very well, then the agreement is made, and is binding forever. We so say."

"Hesperus, not quite. There is a formality we ask you to observe, because it is our custom; and it is a part of the agreement we first made that we honor each other's customs, where they do not violate the other party's nature."

"True. What is the custom?" Hesperus said.

"It is that treaties should be written and signed. We have been unable to think of a way whereby this could be accomplished between us, because our physical natures are so different. Can you help us?"

"Certainly," Hesperus said promptly. "But first you must show me a writing and read it to me, so that I will know your written characters. There is a writing on that wall that seems extensive enough."

Jack turned. On the wall of the chamber behind the rostrum was graven an inscription in Forum capitals. Slowly, he read it aloud:

"They shall beat their swords into plowshares . . . ." His voice broke in the middle of the passage, but he got it back. ". . . Nation shall not raise its hand against nation, neither shall they learn war any more."

"That is ample," Hesperus said. "Now let us similarly inscribe our agreement."

A thin pencil of dazzling white light shot out from him—he was thus identified as the second from the end—and struck the opposite wall, which was blank. Where it touched, smoke rose. Word by word, Hesperus burned into the bare metal, in perfect Forum capitals, the text of that famous document, known today to every school child. It was word for word as Jack Loftus and Gabriel had spoken it in the Coal Sack, which accounts for its curiously informal, conversational style.

"Now," Hesperus said, "we shall sign it. For this we appoint Lucifer, the first of all the Angels on the Earth. Is this your will as well, Jack?"

Jack looked at Nilssen, who nodded vigorously.

"We accept."

The Angel next to Hesperus vanished, and there was a screaming hiss. A moment later he was back.

At the foot of the new document, cut completely through the wall, was the teardrop silhouette of an Angel. It is there still.

"It is completed," Hesperus said. "How will you sign it, we leave to you. Whom do you choose?"

Again Jack turned to Nilssen, who said at once, "Jack, you sign it. It is your creation."

"I can't, sir. I'm not of age. I don't want to introduce any possible trouble for the future over such a little thing."

"Name some one, then," Nilssen said. "They want to hear you do so, obviously. Jack, the honor is plainly yours."

"Thank you," Jack said shakily. He thought a moment. This

had been Secretary Hart's doing, really; he had set it in motion; but the Angels had already set a precedent, and that too had better be honored, for the sake of the future.

"I name Dr. Howard Langer, Earth's first ambassador to the nest . . . if that is your will as well, Hesperus."

"It is wholly appropriate," Hesperus said.

"Dr. Langer, will you sign for humanity . . . if you can figure out some equally drastic way of doing it?"

Langer laughed. "Proudly," he said. He leaned over toward one of Secretary Hart's military aides and plucked his beam gun from its holster. Holding it in both hands—for he was still very shaky—he burned a large signature into the wall next to the silhouette of Lucifer.

"And that," he said, handing the pistol back, "is probably the best use a weapon has ever been put to."

"It is concluded," Hesperus said; and then, suddenly, the big chamber was a tumult of cheers. Jack was dimly aware that Sandbag and Secretary Hart were both pounding him on the back, and that Nilssen and the President were both coming down from the rostrum toward him. There were only two Angels in the room now: Lucifer and Hesperus. Plainly they were waiting for him.

"Hesperus, Lucifer," he said. "Thank you, and let's get out of here."

"Hey, wait!" Sylvia shouted. "Stop! Doggone it, I want an interview!" But for once, she did not have the last word.

"Yes," Hesperus said. "We are well begun, but there is still much to do."

FOR THE FIRST TIME IN PAPERBACK, FOUR
SPACED-OUT FANTASIES OF CHILLING SATIRE
AND MIND-BENDING FUTURISM FROM THE
MODERN MASTER OF SCIENCE FICTION:

THE CYBERIAD   51557 $2.50

The intergalactic capers of two "cosmic constructors"
as they vie to out-invent each other building gargan-
tuan cybernetic monsters all across the universe.

THE FUTUROLOGICAL CONGRESS   52332 $2.25

A traveler from outer space comes to Earth for a conference, but a revolution catapults him into a syn-
thetic future paradise created by hallucinogenic
drugs.

THE INVESTIGATION   29314 $1.50

When dead bodies inexplicably resurrect themselves, a shrewd detective and an adroit statistician
match metaphysical wits in a case that lies beyond
mind, beyond this world.

MEMOIRS FOUND IN A BATHTUB   29959 $1.50

Far in the future a man wanders pointlessly in the
designed destiny of a vast underground labyrinth,
the final stronghold of the American Pentagon.

> **"A major figure who just happens to be a
> science fiction writer ... very likely, he is also the
> bestselling SF writer in the world."**
> *Fantasy and Science Fiction*

LEM 2-81

If you like Heinlein, will you love Van Vogt?

A READER'S GUIDE TO SCIENCE FICTION

by Baird Searles, Martin Last, Beth Meacham, and Michael Franklin

Here is a comprehensive and fascinating source book for every reader of science fiction — from the novice to the discerning devotee. Its invaluable guidance includes:

*A comprehensive listing of over 200 past and present authors, with a profile of the author's style, his works, and other suggested writers the reader might enjoy

*An index to Hugo and Nebula Award winners, in the categories of novel, novelette, and short story

*An outstanding basic reading list highlighting the history and various kinds of science fiction

*A concise and entertaining look at the roots of Science Fiction and the literature into which it has evolved today.

"A clear, well-organized introduction."
<u>Washington Post Book World</u>

"A valuable reference work."
<u>Starship</u>

AVON Paperback

46128 / $2.95

GSciFi 6-81 (2-9)

THE EPIC OF WANDOR
by Roland Green

"Roland Green . . . has mastered the art of writing continuously fresh and picturesque series of character novels . . . entertainment it is."
Chicago Sun-Times

The mighty hero Wandor is given a perilous task by the last of the Five Crowned Kings. He and the beautiful sorceress Gwynna must find five legendary weapons—the Helm of Janar, the Ax of Yevoda, the Spear of Valkath, the Sword of Artos and the Dragon-Steed of Morkol. Their travels take them through magical and monumental battles of flashing swords and fantasy. Their dangerous task must be completed—or peace will never reign in their land again.

WANDOR'S RIDE	45658	$1.95
WANDOR'S JOURNEY	45641	$1.95
WANDOR'S VOYAGE	44271	$1.95
WANDOR'S FLIGHT	77834	$2.75
WANDOR'S BATTLE	Coming soon	